DOWN BUT NOT OUT

It was a long way to the bottom of the desert chasm. It felt like pure hell as Skye rolled down the sloping sides. His hands were bound together. His body felt like it was being torn apart. And above him Aquena and his *bandito* crew were aiming to fill his flesh with lead as they emptied their guns at his free-falling frame.

He could barely hear the gunfire—it was almost obliterated by the pain as he fell, rolled, turned, smashed against one protrusion and then another and kept falling. Then he felt consciousness leaving him as he hit bottom, dimly aware of bullets pinging against nearby rocks before the world disappeared.

All was quiet when he came to. He slowly turned on his side and cried out with the agony of it. He could see up the side of the chasm to the top. The *banditos* were gone. They had assumed he was dead either from the fall or from their bullets. *Wrong, you bastards,* he hissed . . .

. . . and now it was the Trailsman's turn to deal out death. . . .

THE
TRAILSMAN
147

DEATH
TRAILS

by

Jon Sharpe

A SIGNET BOOK

SIGNET
Published by the Penguin Group
Penguin Books USA Inc., 375 Hudson Street,
New York, New York 10014, U.S.A.
Penguin Books Ltd, 27 Wrights Lane,
London W8 5TZ, England
Penguin Books Australia Ltd, Ringwood,
Victoria, Australia
Penguin Books Canada Ltd, 10 Alcorn Avenue,
Toronto, Ontario, Canada M4V 3B2
Penguin Books (N.Z.) Ltd, 182-190 Wairau Road,
Auckland 10, New Zealand

Penguin Books Ltd, Registered Offices:
Harmondsworth, Middlesex, England

First published by Signet, an imprint of Dutton Signet,
a division of Penguin Books USA Inc.

First Printing, March, 1994
10 9 8 7 6 5 4 3 2 1

The first chapter of this book previously appeared in *Nebraska Nightmare*,
the one hundred forty-sixth volume in this series.

   REGISTERED TRADEMARK—MARCA REGISTRADA

Printed in the United States of America

The Trailsman

Beginnings ... they bend the tree and they mark the man. Skye Fargo was born when he was eighteen. Terror was his midwife, vengeance his first cry. Killing spawned Skye Fargo, ruthless, cold-blooded murder. Out of the acrid smoke of gunpowder still hanging in the air, he rose, cried out a promise never forgotten.

The Trailsman they began to call him all across the West: searcher, scout, hunter, the man who could see where others only looked, his skills for hire but not his soul, the man who lived each day to the fullest, yet trailed each tomorrow. Skye Fargo, the Trailsman, the seeker who could take the wildness of a land and the wanting of a woman and make them his own.

*1860, where the Indian territory
of Oklahoma spilled over into Texas
and where deceit spilled over
into death . . .*

1

Fargo had expected trouble during the entire drive. If you had any trail sense you always expected trouble, especially going through the heart of the Oklahoma Indian territory. Then, this drive had other danger signs. There weren't enough cowhands for the size of the herd and half of them were very young and inexperienced. Yet when the trouble came, he didn't expect it. They had perhaps another two days to reach Fort Worth, he estimated, when it happened.

It came in the form of Brad Ales, the foreman of the crew and the man who had hired him. Fargo snapped awake when he heard the footsteps just before dawn and found himself staring into the barrel of a six-shot, single-action Remington-Beals revolver. A face looked down the seven-and-a-half-inch barrel at him, the face of Brad Ales, the half-moon scar on his chin strangely prominent in the last of the moonlight. Two of his men, Johnson and Olmey, stood behind him, also with their guns drawn. "Don't move," Brad Ales whispered.

Fargo ignored the command and rose onto one elbow. "What the hell is this?" He frowned. Ales answered by scooping up the jeans on the ground beside the bedroll and pulling the roll of bills from one pocket.

"It's called getting robbed," the man said. "I'm taking back the money I paid you." Fargo's eyes went to the other two men. They hadn't moved. He flicked a quick glance at his own Colt where it lay in its holster and he measured the distance. Short but not short enough, he cursed silently.

"Get up," Brad Ales ordered.

"You gone crazy?" Fargo frowned.

"I've had enough of the chicken feed Rob Abbot pays. This'll make up for a half-year's work," Ales said and at a nod of his head the other two stepped forward and grabbed Fargo by the arms. Fargo half turned and started to twist away when the butt of the Remington crashed down on the top of his head. He felt himself go down onto his knees as the world was suddenly a foggy, spinning place. He was shaking his head, trying to clear it, when the second blow of the gun slammed into him and he collapsed facedown on the ground.

The world vanished and he knew only a void, a place without sound, sight, or touch. It had all taken but seconds and he had no idea how long he'd lain unconscious but when he woke the new dawn streaked the sky. He sat up slowly, his head throbbing and he felt the lump atop his skull and the streak of sticky, half-dried blood that ran down the side of his face. He sat for a moment, let his thoughts assemble themselves, and heard the sounds of cowhands waking. He pushed to his feet, winced, swayed for a moment, and saw the three young faces staring at him from across the ashes of the supper fire.

"Jesus, Fargo, what happened to you," Al Foster said, his unlined face wreathed in a frown.

"I was bushwhacked, right here," Fargo muttered. "By your boss."

"Brad Ales?" one of the other young hands, Ed Deeze, gasped.

"Him, Johnson, and Olmey," Fargo bit out. "You don't see them around, do you?"

"No, sir," Ed Deeze said as he let his gaze move across the herd.

"They robbed me and hightailed it," Fargo said.

"Jesus, I never figured him for that kind, but then we've only known him since the drive started," the younger man said.

"That goes for all of us," Fargo said as he pulled on clothes. His lake blue eyes were the color of February ice. "I'm going after him . . . all of them," he said.

"Look, I'm sorry for what happened, we all are, but you ride off on us and we're in trouble. We can't bring this herd in without you," Ed Deeze said. Fargo took in their young faces, now filled with apprehension. They were right. Even one rider would make the difference, though he hadn't been hired to ride herd. "Besides, I'd think you'd want to see Rob Abbot about this," Deeze added. "I mean, Brad Ales was his man."

Fargo frowned into space for a moment. The young hand's words made sense. It also gave him a reason to stay other than feeling sorry for the trio. "All right," he said. "Let's get moving. I'll ride lead. You three cover the sides and the rear." He saw the relief flood their faces as they hurried away and he saddled the Ovaro, his head still hurting, and rode the magnificent pinto to the head of the steers. He looked back, waved, and Deeze and the other young hands began to move the steers forward. They traveled only an hour when he found a shallow stream that let the cattle drink as he cleaned the caked blood from his face. Later, moving the herd southward again, he thought of how Brad Ales had hired him.

The man had sought him out at the hotel in Wichita where he'd had a needed three-day rest after trail-breaking a large herd from far north in Nebraska Territory for Matt Dreiser. "Dreiser told me you were staying here," Brad Ales had said. "I need a trailsman for a small herd I'm taking to Fort Worth, five hundred steers but all fancy stock. I'm paying five hundred dollars."

Fargo had let a low whistle escape his lips. "That's a lot of money for that short a drive," he remarked.

"Yes, but it's all through Indian territory and I don't want to make that trip on my own," Brad Ales said. "I've all the rest of my hands. You're the last one and I'm told you're the best. Pay up front."

"Five hundred dollars," Fargo murmured silently. It was an offer too good to turn down and he'd had a good rest. He'd accepted, pocketed the money, and they had started the drive south the next morning. He noticed, during the drive, that Brad Ales, Johnson, and Olmey stayed pretty much to themselves. They gave their three young, inexperienced hands little instruction in handling a herd and there was none of the kind of working camaraderie that developed on most drives. But that wasn't his concern and he spent most of the days riding far ahead of the herd as he broke trail.

Now it was clear that he should have paid more attention, but at the time he'd simply decided Brad Ales wasn't much of a trail foreman. His brow continued to furrow as he rode. There had been something strange about the bushwhacking. Ales could have killed him. It would have eliminated pursuit and he had the chance to do so? Why hadn't he? Most bushwhackers would have and Brad Ales had the cruelty in his face for it. Yet he hadn't. The anomaly stayed with Fargo as he rode until he finally put it aside and concentrated on the terrain in front of him. It was mostly flat but a line of low sandstone dunes rose up at his right. They were drawing close enough to Fort Worth and he had all but dismissed any further chance of Indian trouble. They'd been lucky in that regard and suddenly he reined to a halt and his lips drew back in a grimace.

A line of unshod pony prints leading to the sandstone dunes crossed his path. Fargo swung from the Ovaro and knelt on the ground. He pressed his fingers into the tracks and swore silently. Nothing dry and crumbling about them. They were firm and fresh, not more than a few hours old, he guessed as he returned to the saddle. Dismissing Indian trouble had been premature, a case of wishful thinking. He turned the horse around and slowly rode back to the herd.

Ed Deeze and the other two young men came forward to meet him, their eyes questioning. "Trouble, maybe, Indian pony prints ahead," Fargo said.

"How many?" Deeze questioned.

"Can't say for sure. They were riding single-file and left overlapping prints," Fargo said. "Six to eight, I'd guess."

"You think they'll come after the herd?" Deeze asked.

"Only to stampede them and pick us off," Fargo said.

Deeze winced. "If they stampede we'll never round them up."

"That depends," Fargo said and Deeze frowned. "Nobody can completely control a stampede but we can do some things."

"Like what?" Deeze questioned.

"They'll try to stampede the herd off in all directions. That's what we don't want," Fargo said.

"How do we stop that?"

"We stampede them," Fargo said and saw the younger man's brows lift. "That'll give us some control. We set them off running together and they'll pretty much stay together. That's the way with cattle. We stay with them until they run themselves out."

"If we can stay alive," Deeze mumbled.

"Right," Fargo said. "Spread out and move them." He took a position just behind the center of the herd while the three younger men moved outward. It was a small herd and Fargo was grateful for that. They'd be more inclined to stay together having traveled as a cohesive unit. The big, sprawling herds never did develop any unity. Fargo's eyes swept the sandstone formations as they drove the cattle forward. If the Indians were behind the sandstone they could be Wichita, Osage, or even Kiowa. The Kiowa had a habit of ranging far and wide. But they could also be Comanche. He hoped not.

They were reaching the end of the sandstone formations when the barely clad horsemen swept into sight, a thousand or so yards ahead of them. Eight, he counted, as they crossed in front of the approaching herd and he glimpsed one brave wearing a full-beaded choker with a tie decorated with Osage markings. Fargo was grateful for that. An Osage arrow could kill you as dead as a Comanche arrow but he'd do battle with the Osage over the Comanche anytime. He glanced to his side and saw Ed Deeze and the others watching him. "Stay low in the saddle and stay with the herd. Don't drop back. Run inside them if you

14

have to," Fargo said as he drew his colt. "Now let's send them."

He raised the revolver and sent a scattershot pattern of bullets into the air and heard Deeze and the other two men do the same. The sudden sharp explosion of sound at their very backs was all the cattle needed. With a roar of bellowing sound they stampeded straight ahead, a mass of thundering hoofs and horns. Fargo spurred the Ovaro with them, riding at the very heels of the racing steers as he flattened himself in the saddle. He saw the Osage wheel their ponies and race off to both sides of the stampeding herd. A quick glance showed Ed Deeze and the other two young hands keeping up with the steers, also low in their saddles. Fargo fought the bounce of the galloping horse under him as he reloaded. When he raised the Colt again he steadied his hand, waited, let one of the Osage come into his sights and fired.

The Osage flew from his pony and Fargo swung the Colt, found another target, and fired. The attacker tried to turn away but he was too late and the heavy bullet tore his side open. Fargo saw him disappear from view and he ducked lower as two rifle shots tore over his head. A few of the Osage had rifles but most were firing arrows as they gathered themselves to race alongside the stampeding herd. Fargo saw another go down but not from his gun and he pressed the Ovaro forward through a space that opened up between two steers. He could see the three young heads still bobbing up and down amid the racing steers and he glimpsed an Osage drop back to swing in behind him. He half turned in the saddle, the Colt raised as he clung to the reins with one hand. The Indian came into sight swinging his pony around to bring up at the rear of the herd. Fargo fired just as the Ovaro swerved to avoid colliding with one of the steers. The brave clutched at his shoulder but managed to stay on his pony as he turned away.

Fargo returned his attention to staying with the still-racing steers, then brought the Ovaro back a pace as the cattle closed ranks in front of him. He glimpsed Ed Deeze off to his right but hadn't time to look for the others as he had to again pull away from the swerving cattle. But they were slowing, he saw, and for the most part, still together. They continued to slow, losing wind and power, panic fading with tired muscles. Fargo saw Ed Deeze, then the other two hands, rise in their saddles. His gaze swept past them to where the Osage were riding away, unwilling to lose more warriors in what had been, from the start, something less than a deadly attack. Once again, Fargo was glad they had not been the Comanche.

"Cover the flanks," he called out to Deeze. "Keep them together so they don't wander off." He let the Ovaro fall back and then raced the horse around the edge of the slowing herd until he was ahead of them. He rode back and forth in front of the lead steers and saw them slow further and finally come to a halt, breathing heavily. He heard Ed Deeze's shouts as he herded straying steers back to the main herd and finally there was only the heavy breathing of the cattle as they stood still. "We were lucky," Fargo said to Ed Deeze as the younger man rode up to him.

"Stampeding the herd at them took them by surprise. They never got untracked," Deeze said.

Fargo's eyes moved across the herd. "Let them rest for an hour and then move them slowly. I'll ride on," he said and moved the Ovaro away at a walk. The Oklahoma terrain stayed mostly flat as he rode on, his eyes scanning the ground. But he found no new pony prints, and after one more night, they were driving the herd into Forth Worth. He asked questions, found the Rob Abbot spread at the south end of town—three big corrals and a cluster of warehouses, stables, and a large, slate-shingled main house. Corral hands opened the gates as the three young hands drove the herd inside. "Where do I find Rob Abbot?" Fargo asked one of the men.

"In the main house," the man said. "I'm sure he's watched you ride in."

Fargo nodded and rode to the slate-roofed house where a man stepped outside as he rode to a halt and dismounted. Fargo took in a tall man, perhaps fifty, he guessed, with hair still dark, an angled face with dark and piercing eyes, a prominent nose that, with the piercing eyes, gave him a somewhat hawklike expression. "Rob Abbot?" Fargo asked.

"That's right," the man said. "Who are you?"

"Skye Fargo."

Rob Abbot frowned. "Fargo ... the one they call the Trailsman? I've heard of you," he said.

"I'd think so, seeing as how you hired me," Fargo said.

Robert Abbot frowned back. "What are you talking about? I never hired you."

"You told Brad Ales to hire me," Fargo said.

"I never told him to hire you or anyone else but some cowhands," the man said and Fargo felt the stab of apprehension inside himself. "By the way, where is Brad? I didn't see him ride in with you."

"He's gone. He bushwhacked me, stole back the money he'd paid me, and lit out, along with Johnson and Olmey," Fargo said.

Rob Abbot stared at him. "By God, I do believe you're telling me the truth," the man said.

"Damn right I'm telling you the truth," Fargo snapped.

"Maybe you'd better come inside," Abbot said and Fargo followed him into the living room of the house and saw a large room with a leather sofa and leather chairs, stone walls hung with Indian blankets and old muskets, a comfortable room. Abbot turned to face him with a quizzical glance, his piercing eyes probing. "You've come looking to me. You were thinking it was my responsibility because I had him hire you," he said.

"Something like that," Fargo said.

"Only it's not. I never hired you, never told him to. I hire anyone they have a piece of paper with my name on it," the man said.

"He worked for you," Fargo tried.

"That doesn't make me responsible for every damn thing he does," Abbot countered and Fargo's lips tightened as he had to agree with the man's reply. "But I can put together why he bushwhacked you," Abbot said.

"I'd like to hear that," Fargo said.

"He's been unhappy here lately. He asked me for a bonus if he got the herd here early, by next week. I agreed and he asked me for the money up front, said it'd make him feel better, said he wanted the feel of it in his pocket."

"You agreed again."

"Yes. He'd worked for me for a year. If it'd help make him get the herd here early I was willing to go along with it," Abbot said. "It's plain now that he used the money to hire you and then stole it back from you."

"That's what the son of a bitch did," Fargo said. "But two questions bother me. Why'd he wait till I was only two days from here and could bring the herd in?"

Abbot smiled. "That's easy. He knew if I had the herd I'd no cause to go chasing after him."

"Then why didn't he kill me. Most bushwhackers would have?" Fargo questioned.

"That's easy, too. If he was to be caught, robbin' brings a lot less jail than murder," Abbot said.

Fargo let out a deep sigh. Abbot was right on everything. "Which all means you've got your cattle and I've got empty pockets," he said.

"I'm sorry for that but I'm still not responsible for what happened but I'd like to help you out. Fact is, maybe we can do each other a turn," Abbot said, his lips pursing in thought. "I've a job for a man with your skills and I'll pay real good money, more than enough to pay for the time you've lost and for what Brad Ales stole back from you."

"I'm listening," Fargo said.

"I want you to find my daughter and bring her back here to me," the man said.

Fargo thought for a moment. "I'm not much for tracking down runaways," he said.

"But you have tracked down people."

"I have."

"And it's more than that," Abbot said.

"How old is she?" Fargo asked.

"Twenty-two," Abbot said.

"Then she's old enough to do what she wants. I'd need a reason to haul her back," Fargo said.

"She stole two thousand dollars from me when she left. That'll do for a reason."

"It will for a sheriff but not for me. What's the real story?" Fargo queried. "Why do you want her back?"

Rob Abbot motioned him to come to the large window at one side of the room. "Look out there. That's Abbot Enterprises. We buy and sell cattle. Horses, too, and hogs. We run a freight line. We own storage depots. We operate two riverboats that sail the Trinity to Galveston and back and they're always loaded. It's a fine enterprise that makes good money but it's going down the drain because of Dulcy."

"How's that?" Fargo inquired.

"Because I need her signature on every important document, on bank withdrawals, checks, credit transactions, everything. You see, the business was really my wife's, Dulcy's mother, a family business. When Clara died she wanted Dulcy to be a part of the business so she made Dulcy a partner in her will. But Dulcy never gave a damn about the business. She told me to sell out or she'd bring the whole thing down. I thought she was just talking until I found out differently."

"But she's bringing it down on her head, too. Seems like she's cutting her nose off to spite her face," Fargo said.

"She was left a small income of her own, enough to get by," Abbot said. "She's also chasing a man, a gambler who ditched her. But she still wants him. This is a terrible thing for a father to say but Dulcy is a spoiled, unprincipled, vicious young woman who's capable of anything. I've often wondered if she wasn't more than a little twisted inside."

"You sure make her sound that way," Fargo said.

"Now you know why I have to have her brought back here and as damn soon as possible," Abbot said.

"I could bring her back and she might still refuse to sign," Fargo said.

"I think once she's back here she'll sign. She always has. If not, I'll make her an offer to buy her out. I'm sure she'll go for that. But I need her here, first, and time to convince her to do what's right," the man said. "I'll pay you a thousand, half up front, the rest when you bring her in."

Fargo felt his brows lift. "That'll pay for a lot of tracking," he said. "But I still aim to get Brad Ales. He set me up, bushwhacked me, and robbed me. I don't take to any of those things much less all three together."

"I want you to forget about Brad Ales. You concentrate on finding Dulcy," Rob Abbot said.

"You send anyone else after her?" Fargo questioned.

"No. I thought she might come back on her own. I guessed wrong," Abbot said.

"How long has she been gone?"

"Three months. I had enough cash on hand to last that long," the man said.

"What's she look like?" Fargo asked.

"Tall, brown hair, brown eyes, good-looking enough," Abbot said.

"That'd fit a lot of girls," Fargo sniffed.

"I know," Abbot shrugged helplessly. "I've one lead. She had a woman friend who lived in Kempton. She might've gone there."

"That's a start," Fargo said.

"She has one favorite expression. When she gets real mad at somebody she says they're lower than snake shit," Abbot said.

"Everything helps. This gambler she's chasing. What's his name?" Fargo asked.

"I'm not sure. She never did tell me. It was always a sore point with us," the man said.

"All right, you've got a deal, mister," Fargo said. "And a herd of cattle."

"I thank you for the second one and I'm sure I'll be thanking you for the first," Abbot said. "Now I'll get your money." He hurried into another room and Fargo glimpsed what seemed to be a small office with a desk and file cabinet. He returned in moments with the roll of crisp bills that Fargo stuffed into an inside pocket in his vest. "Good luck. Time's important," Abbot said as he walked to the door with Fargo. "One last thing, and I hate to even bring this up, but I know how vicious Dulcy can be. If anything should happen to her, I mean anything real bad, I want you to bring her body back here anyway. Her mother would want her buried here on our land."

"Understood," Fargo said and strode to his horse. He rode from the Abbot layout digesting everything that had been told him. It had been quite a story. Rob Abbot plainly had little love left for his daughter but a lot of need for her. From his words, Dulcy Abbot was a handful of hellcat. Kempton lay southwest but Fargo sent the pinto north. Despite Abbot's instructions, he still wanted to cross paths with Brad Ales again and he took the time to return to where the herd had halted that night. It was the next morning when he finally reached the spot, just north of the small stream. He had no trouble finding the hoofprints of the three horses that had raced away to the northeast and he followed at a slow, steady trot, more hope than expectation inside him.

But hope brought its own rewards as, some half-dozen miles on, he saw the footprints turn south and stay southward. Fargo allowed himself a small smile of satisfaction. With a little luck he could settle a score of his own while pursuing a hellcat named Dulcy. He smiled again at the incongruity of the name and the young woman Rob Abbot had described. But he had learned long ago that this was a world of incongruities. He just hadn't tracked one before now.

2

Kempton lay directly south, across the Leon River, but there were three derelict towns along the way, each made up of a saloon and a few buildings, hardscrabble places populated by hardscrabble people. He paused at each to ask the same question at each saloon and the bartender at the third place gave him the answer he wanted. "Three of them, one with a half-moon scar on his chin? Yep, they were here a day or two ago," the man said.

"They say which way they were headed?" Fargo asked.

"One of them talked about Zaragoza," the bartender said.

"Much obliged," Fargo nodded and rode on with the grim smile renewed inside him. He had guessed right. Ales was making for the border. But he wasn't hurrying, confident he was away free and clear. He had a surprise in store, Fargo murmured inwardly. Fargo rode through the Texas terrain. It was hot and mostly dry, with cactus and yucca and spotted spurges. Sandstone formations as old as the earth itself rose in stark beauty. When he stopped at a shallow stream to let the pinto drink he saw unshod pony prints, none fresh. He had no need to wonder about tribes, now. He'd gone far enough south to be in Comanche territory and he rode on with his eyes scanning the terrain with new caution.

Kempton came into sight a day later, no major town but a good deal more substantial than the other three he'd passed through. Rob Abbot had said that Dulcy had a friend here and there was a good chance she may have stayed awhile. There was even a far-out chance she could still be here, he mused as he rode the Ovaro slowly down the wide main street of the town. It was logical she would have stayed with her friend but he drew to a halt before an inn, dismounted, and went inside where an elderly, stooped man in shirtsleeves and a red armband greeted him.

"Looking for a young lady and I wondered if she might have stayed here," Fargo said.

"When would she have stopped here?" the clerk asked.

"Maybe three months back. Name's Dulcy Abbot," Fargo said and saw the man's face seem to grow longer as his brows lifted.

"Dulcy?" the man echoed. "That sweet, wonderful person?"

"I guess so," Fargo said, taken aback for a moment.

The man's face lengthened still further. "Everybody in town is sorry she had to leave us," he said.

"She left? You know where I might find her?" Fargo questioned.

The man let his lips purse in thought for a moment. "I think you'd better speak to Sheriff Timkins about that," he said.

"The sheriff?" Fargo frowned. "I thought you said she was a sweet, wonderful person."

"Oh yes, indeed, that's Dulcy. But you'd best go see the sheriff. That's all I'm going to say, friend," the man said.

Fargo shrugged as he left the inn and walked down the street, the Ovaro following, until he spied the sign that read SHERRIF over the door of a narrow frame building. He peered through the window to see the man seated inside behind a wood desk, short, graying, a little portly, a face totally unremarkable, the star-shaped badge on his shirt. He looked up as Fargo entered.

"Just came from the inn. Man there said I should see you. I'm looking for Dulcy Abbot," Fargo said and watched a sudden awareness slide across the man's placid face.

"And who might you be, stranger?" the sheriff asked.

"Name's Fargo ... Skye Fargo."

"What brings you looking for Dulcy?" Sheriff Timkins asked.

"Her pa sent me to bring her home," Fargo answered.

"He did? Well now, we can all understand why he'd want her home, a warm, sweet, sharing person like Dulcy," the sheriff said. Fargo frowned inwardly. He was getting a very different description of Dulcy Abbot from the one her father had given.

"Then you can tell me where I'll find her. I take it she's still in town," Fargo said.

Sheriff Timkins's plain face grew suddenly doleful. "I guess you could say that," he murmured.

"What's that mean?" Fargo queried and heard the growing impatience in his voice.

"Poor sweet, wonderful Dulcy is dead," the sheriff said.

Fargo found himself staring in astonishment at the sheriff. "Dead?" he echoed.

"She took a sudden, terrible fever and died in a

25

matter of days. The doc couldn't do a thing for her," the sheriff said. Fargo continued to stare as the sheriff's words swirled around him, a shatteringly unexpected twist to things. "I'm sorry to have to tell you like this, like a slap of cold water in the face. But we all loved Dulcy here, everybody did," the man said.

"When did this happen?" Fargo queried.

"Only a week ago," the sheriff said.

"Did you figure to get in touch with her pa?" Fargo questioned.

The sheriff looked suddenly uncomfortable. "We talked about it," he said.

"You talked about it?" Fargo frowned.

"Well, you see Dulcy told us she'd never been happy at home. She felt Kempton was her home now and we all were her family," the sheriff said.

"And she's buried here?" Fargo asked.

"Yes, right here in our cemetery just outside town. Would you like to see her resting place?" the man said.

Fargo thought for a moment. "Yes, I would. It'll let me tell her pa I saw it with my own eyes," he decided.

"Follow me," the sheriff said as he led the way from the office and down the street. He paused at a general store, one half of the building showing charred wood, the other half obviously rebuilt with new planking. A man in a shopkeeper's apron came from the store, thin and slight of build with steel-rimmed spectacles on a long, narrow face. "This here is Skye Fargo," the sheriff introduced. "He's come here looking to find Dulcy. Tell him what she did for you, Ben."

The storekeeper half smiled in wistful remembrance. "Ben Simpson, Fargo. A fire burned down half my store and I just didn't have the cash to rebuild and restock. Dulcy loaned me three hundred dollars for everything I needed to do. That's the kind of person she was," the man said.

"Here comes Madge Brophy," Sheriff Timkins cut in as a wide-hipped, matronly woman came along. "Madge, can you stop a minute?" the sheriff called. "This gent came looking for Dulcy. We're on our way to the cemetery now."

"I just came from there," Madge Brophy said.

"Tell Mr. Fargo what Dulcy did for you," Sheriff Timkins said.

"Just nursed me back from death's door when I took sick and paid Doc Elkhorn every bill he sent," the woman said. "She was an exceptional young woman. Ask anybody in this town about that. Ask Howie Altpack. She gave him money to buy a new team of horses when he lost his in that stable fire. There's nobody in this town she hasn't helped."

"Thanks, Madge. We have to get on to the cemetery," the sheriff said.

"I'll go back with you. Nothing wrong in saying another prayer," Madge Brophy said.

"I'll come along, too," Ben Simpson chimed in and both he and the woman fell in step behind Fargo and the sheriff. Again, Fargo couldn't fit this young woman with the one her father had described. Maybe Rob Abbot simply had a lousy relationship with his daughter, who seemed to have been a very different person with everyone else. A few more townspeople joined the small group on the way to the cemetery as the sheriff called out to them and finally Fargo found himself standing beside a gravesite, an unmarked headstone in place.

"We haven't had time to get the headstone properly engraved yet, seeing as how it only happened last week," the sheriff said. "But we'll be getting to that real soon."

"That's real good of you folks," Fargo said as his eyes narrowed as they swept the soil of the gravesite and lingered at the edges where the headstone was planted into the ground. "I'll just pay a moment of respect, if you don't mind," he said and dropped to one knee, his head bowed. But his eyes were peering at the soil where it came against the headstone. Something was wrong, he muttered silently. The headstone hadn't been put in place a week ago. The soil around it was dry and crumbly. Maybe two months ago, he guessed, and he let one hand press down on the soil of the gravesite. It was bone dry and he pressed harder though he seemed not to move a muscle. There wasn't any give to the soil. It had also been in place for a lot longer than a week.

He rose to his feet and allowed a respectful smile to reach out to the sheriff and the others. "You folks have sure done a fine, Christian job," he said and everyone seemed modestly pleased. "I understand Dulcy had a friend here in town. I'd like to talk to her before I go back," he said.

"That'd be Mary Coulter," Sheriff Timkins said. "She lives at the end of town. I'll take you to her."

"Obliged," Fargo said as he followed the sheriff from the cemetery. The others dropped away as the sheriff led him through town to a small house of plain, unpainted clapboard where a young woman opened the door, a face as plain as her house, a portly body beneath it.

"This here is Skye Fargo. He wants to talk to you about Dulcy," the sheriff said.

"Her pa sent you?" Mary Coulter asked.

"He did," Fargo nodded.

28

"Dulcy knew he'd send somebody. She never wanted to go back, you know. She won't have to now. Fate took care of that," Mary Coulter said.

"It seems so," Fargo said, his eyes sharp on her and he caught the brief glance she shot at him before she composed her face again. "She live with you while she was here?" he asked.

"Yes, most of the time," the young woman said.

"About how long was that?" Fargo questioned.

Mary Coulter shrugged. "Never counted. About three months, I'd guess."

"Everybody speaks real highly of her," he commented.

"Of course. Dulcy was a wonderful person. It's just a rotten shame the way things turned out," she said.

"Any messages for her pa?" Fargo inquired blandly.

"Tell him Dulcy's at peace and now he can stop searching for her," Mary Coulter said.

"I'll do that," Fargo said and left the young woman with an agreeable smile. But when he led the Ovaro down the street as dusk descended, his lake blue eyes were narrowed. The stories were consistent in events, time, and Dulcy's warm character. But there was something wrong, he murmured inwardly. Something was wrong, a silent voice told him. Fargo believed in the power of silent voices. The hoofprints on a trail, the feel of the sod, the broken end of a branch, the bruised leaves of a bush, they were all silent voices and he had long ago learned to listen to their messages. He would listen to one more in this strange little town.

Dusk had given way to night when he halted at the general store and went inside. Ben Simpson hurried over to greet him. "I'm afraid there's nothing more I can tell you, Fargo," he said almost apologetically.

"This is a different kind of visit. I'm here as a customer," Fargo smiled. "I need a shovel, not too long a handle. Mine broke and I always like to keep a shovel with me when I'm on a long trip."

"Got some short-handled ones right here," Simpson said and Fargo chose one at random and went on his way. Outside, he cast a glance at the night sky. A three-quarter moon. He wouldn't need a lantern, he decided, nor did he want to use one. He walked on to the saloon in the middle of town where they were featuring Buffalo steaks at half-price with a drink. He ordered, ate leisurely, and when he finished he sauntered to the bar. The bartender, a man with silvered hair but still powerful arms and shoulders, took him in with a practiced eye.

"Just passing through?" the man asked.

"That's right. I'm looking for three men, one with a scar on his chin," Fargo said. "They pass this way?"

"They did. I remember the one with the scar. About two days back," the bartender said and Fargo smiled inwardly. His luck was still holding. "I thought you were the one who came looking for Dulcy Abbot," the barkeep said.

"I am," Fargo said and caught the moment of surprise in the man's eyes. "Don't tell me Dulcy was one of your customers," he remarked.

"No, she wasn't but I was on the committee to build a proper town hall. I'll always remember how generous she was as well as being a fine young lady," the man said.

One more of Dulcy's admirers, Fargo grunted to himself. There seemed no end to them in Kempton. But there was still something wrong.

When he left the saloon the night was still and deep. He walked, the Ovaro behind him, through the silent town to the cemetery and made his way to the gravesite the sheriff had shown him. He paused, the shovel in hand, and once again felt the ground, this time running his hands along the soil at the edges of the headstone. A grim grunt escaped his lips as he pushed to his feet and began to dig.

He worked carefully and neatly, digging open the grave until he had a mound of dirt piled to one side and he stared down at the simple, pine box. He frowned and felt himself wondering if he had misread signs as he flattened himself at the edge of the rectangular hole. A wave of distaste swept over him. Was he being a desecrator, a violator of final privacies? He cursed softly as he reached down and got his fingers under the edge of the lid of the coffin. He tugged and it lifted. It hadn't been nailed shut and he was grateful for that. Still feeling blasphemous, he pulled the coffin lid all the way open and stared down at the empty box. Leaving the lid open, he pushed back from the hole and sat up, his brow creased with a deep furrow.

One question swirled through his mind before all others. Why this elaborate conspiracy? A town had banded together to create a lie, carrying it all the way to a false grave with a headstone in place. He felt the anger gathering inside himself at the very magnitude of the deception. What still remained was the first question. Had they banded together to help Dulcy because she had so won their hearts? Fargo grimaced. There was an air of unreality about that. Saints came few and far between and he'd never met any. But he had met a clever, lying sheriff who was going to come up with the truth.

Fargo made his way back through the town to the sheriff's office and circled to the rear of the building where he found a second doorway and two windows.

He peered into one and managed to make out a furnished living room. The sheriff lived behind his office and jail, as was the case with most small-town sheriffs. Fargo lifted the base of the window and felt it slide upward. Working quietly and carefully, he raised the window enough to let himself climb into the room, where he paused, listening. The sound of raspy but steady breathing came to his ears and he stepped down a short corridor to a second room where he saw the bed and the dark shape atop it.

He crossed to the bed as he unholstered his Colt and halting, he pressed the gun barrel against Sheriff Timkins's temple. The touch of cold steel made the man's eyes snap open, blink, and focus on the big figure standing at his bedside. "Fargo," the sheriff gasped.

"In person," Fargo said, stepped back a pace, and moved the gun barrel from the man's temple. "Get up."

"What in hell do you think you're doing?" Sheriff Timkins growled as he swung from the bed wearing only the bottoms of pajamas. "What's this all about?"

"It's about going for a little walk. Get dressed," Fargo said.

"You realize I can have you clapped in jail for this?" the man said as he began to dress. "You gone out of your mind, mister?"

"We're going to find that out," Fargo said and kept the Colt trained on the sheriff as the man finished dressing. "You won't need your gun. It'll only get you in trouble," he said.

"You're the one in trouble, mister," Sheriff Timkins barked but he obeyed as Fargo motioned to the door with the Colt. Fargo followed close behind Timkins as the man went outside.

"Keep walking, to the end of town," Fargo said, pressing the Colt into the man's back. The sheriff decided to be silent and set a brisk pace. Fargo cast a glance behind him and saw the Ovaro following and as they reached the cemetery, Fargo saw the sheriff slow down at once. Fargo pushed the gun barrel harder into the man's back until they reached the open gravesite and came to a halt. Timkins stared down at the grave and the empty casket inside it.

"I don't see Dulcy Abbot in there. I don't see anybody in there, do you?" Fargo said.

"No, but I . . . I don't understand this, either," the sheriff said.

Fargo half smiled at the man's quick, nervous glance. "Don't bullshit me anymore. I've a short fuse."

"Dammit, you wouldn't shoot a sheriff, Fargo," Timkins said.

"I wouldn't like to," Fargo said with a touch of ruefulness in his voice. "A sheriff's supposed to set an example not be the biggest liar in town."

"I told you, I can't explain this," Timkins said, growing more boldly defensive. He'd need more convincing, Fargo saw. Fargo's left fist shot out with the speed of a rattler's strike. It caught Timkins flush on the point of his jaw and the man flew backward into the open grave and landed in the casket. Fargo stepped to the edge of the grave and peered down as Timkins lay still for a moment, then shook his head to clear it and realized where he was. He started to leap up when Fargo's shot tore through the wood of the pine box an inch from his head. He fell back to lie still in the casket. "Jesus, Fargo, you are crazy," he said.

"Being lied to makes me very angry," Fargo said. "You've one more chance to start talking."

"Look, I don't know," Timkins said, starting to sit up again. "Let me out of here and we'll go back to town and find out what all this means." Fargo sighed as he fired again and Timkins fell back flat in the casket with a curse. Fargo reached down and slammed the lid of the casket shut, then jumped down on top of it. Using the shovel, he began to scoop the dirt back over the pine box. "Jesus, what are you doing?" Timkins called out as he heard the soil dropping onto the casket lid, his voice muffled from inside the box.

"You folks went to all the trouble of digging a grave, putting up a headstone, and sinking an empty casket. I think somebody ought to be there," Fargo said as he continued to shovel.

"No, Jesus, stop," Timkins shouted and Fargo felt the lid of the casket move as the man tried to push it open. But still standing atop it, Fargo's weight held it closed and soon he had enough dirt shoveled back into the grave to keep the lid on. Timkins was screaming now, his voice growing more and more muffled. "No, God, stop it . . . no, no," he yelled.

"I can just about hear you," Fargo said as he tossed another shovelful of dirt onto the pine box.

"Let me out. Jesus, I'll tell you everything. Please, Fargo, Jesus, I can't breathe," the voice came from beneath the dirt.

Fargo stepped down onto the casket again and began to shovel the dirt away, not hurrying, and when he had enough cleared away he climbed from the grave and pulled the casket lid open. Timkins, gasping, all color drained from his face, looked appropriately dead, Fargo thought, as he scrambled out of the pine box. Fargo stepped back and let the man pull himself from the grave where he lay drawing in deep gasps of air as the color finally returned to his face. Timkins finally looked up and pushed to his feet.

"Talk or you'll go back in and you'll stay this time," Fargo said, his voice hard. "Where's Dulcy Abbot?"

"Gone," the man said.

"Where?"

"Blackwood. She was going to Blackwood, she said," the sheriff answered.

"Why'd this whole damn town stick together to cover for her?" Fargo questioned.

"Because she was good to us. She did all the things we told you about," the sheriff said.

"What else did she tell you?"

"That she was running away from her pa and he'd send someone after her. She told us he was a bad man," Timkins said.

"And so she got you all to go along with the story of her being dead," Fargo supplied.

"Yes, that was her idea. She hoped it'd put an end to her pa trying to track her down," Timkins said. "We thought it was the least we could do, seeing as all the good things she'd done for us. We were happy to help her."

Fargo grunted with amazement. Dulcy had spent some of the two thousand dollars she'd taken from her pa to buy the help of the whole damn town. She'd presented a picture of a warm, sweet young woman desperately running from an unhappy home. Maybe Dulcy Abbot wasn't the young woman her father had described but she wasn't the warm, selfless character she'd coaxed the town into believing she was. With the right combination of charm, sympathetic appeal, and money, she had cleverly masterminded the entire elaborate deception. Dulcy Abbot was becoming not only more of a challenge but a damn sight more intriguing.

"How long ago did you dig that grave?" Fargo questioned.

"About a month ago," the man said and had the good manners to sound sheepish about it.

"That's when Dulcy really left you," Fargo said and Timkins nodded. "Get out of here and try to remember you're a sheriff and a sheriff's supposed to uphold truth not a pack of lies," Fargo said as he strode to where the Ovaro waited and swung into the saddle.

"You're doing the wrong thing chasing after that fine young woman, Fargo. She's just trying to get away from a terrible home," Timkins called after him.

"I'll be finding that out for myself, thank you," Fargo said and put the Ovaro into a canter. Dulcy had certainly done a job on the townsfolk, he murmured silently, not without respect for her. She would have gotten away with the deception if Rob Abbot had sent an ordinary man to track her down. Only the eye of the trailsman made him pick up those little things that told him something was wrong. But then that's why Abbot had hired him. He also apparently respected Dulcy's abilities, perhaps with more reason than he'd let on, Fargo mused as the Ovaro crossed over a low hill and down the other side.

The first gray-pink streaks of the new day were beginning to spear the horizon sky and he felt the tiredness settling over him. He found a shady spot under the arch of a rock formation and was asleep when the morning came. He finally woke to find the sun almost in the noon sky. He found a tiny pond, washed, and let the Ovaro drink before he set out again. Blackwood was not a town he'd ever visited but he knew it lay south on an almost direct line. His eyes swept the flat land, the low hills, and sandstone rocks that glowed a burnished gold under the sun as unshod pony prints continued to dot the ground. It took two days' riding to reach the town and it was dusk when he moved down the main street. Not as centered as Kempton, it took up more land and gave a slightly seedier appearance.

He halted at a frame building that needed a new coat of paint where a sign read THE BLACKWOOD BED & BOARD HOUSE. Inside the house, a middle-aged woman greeted him from behind a desk and register ledger. She offered a pleasant smile and eyes that were friendly behind horn-rimmed spectacles. "I'm trying to find someone," Fargo began. "I thought perhaps she might be living here. Her name's Dulcy Abbot."

"Dulcy? That sweet, warm, wonderful girl?" the woman gushed.

Christ, not again, Fargo muttered silently.

3

Fargo swallowed the words and his immediate reaction to fasten the woman with a slightly jaundiced stare. "Does sweet, wonderful Dulcy still live here?" he asked.

"Oh no, she only stayed here a week," the woman said.

"That figures," Fargo mumbled and started to turn away.

"She's been living in one of the cabins Sid Bream rents just outside town," the woman said and he halted and turned back, his eyes widening.

"You mean, she's still here in Blackwood?" he questioned.

"Yes, a lovely girl, always pleasant, always helpful," the woman said.

"I know all about that side of her. Where do I find Sid Bream" Fargo cut in.

"With his cabins, just past the south end of town. He lives in the first one," the woman said and Fargo tossed her an appreciative nod as he strode from the room. He rode from town minutes later and saw the six small cabins in a loose cluster beyond the town proper. He allowed himself a grim smile. Dulcy had made her first mistake, one of overconfidence. She was plainly so certain her careful deception would turn away anyone who was sent after her she'd not bothered to go further than Blackwood. A man came out as he halted before the first cabin, grizzled hair and grizzled beard and wearing only overalls.

"Looking for Dulcy Abbot," Fargo said.

"Cabin 6, the last one. You'll see a bay gelding outside," Sid Bream answered and cast him a quizzical glance. "Who be you? She hasn't had any visitors before this," the man asked.

"An old family friend," Fargo said and moved the Ovaro past the cabins, all very much the same, solid log construction with shingled roofs. He spotted the bay gelding, came to a halt at the cabin, and dismounted. The door was opened at his knock and he took in the young woman standing there in a blue dress with a scoop neck. Somehow, she wasn't what he'd expected, though he hadn't formed any real picture in his mind. The brown hair and brown eyes were there but she was softer, a sweet face more pleasant than pretty, a body also softly curved, perhaps ten unneeded pounds on it and not quite as tall as he'd expected. Her brown eyes hadn't any of the fire and sharpness of a young woman who'd so carefully orchestrated everything that took place in Kempton. "Dulcy Abbot?" he queried.

Her eyes regarded him for a moment, narrowing ever so slightly. "Who wants to know?" she returned.

"Skye Fargo," he said.

"Who's Skye Fargo?"

"The man your pa sent to fetch you back," Fargo said and this time her brown eyes widened in a moment of surprise.

"I see," she said slowly. "My compliments. You must be very good."

"My compliments to you. That was a damn good show you put on in Kempton," Fargo said.

"I think you'd better come inside," she said and he followed her into the cabin, his eyes taking in a very round rear that moved with a soft rhythm. Inside the cabin, he found himself in a compact room with a small sofa and a heavy wood table against one wall. He saw a second room through a doorway with a curtain pulled back. "Please sit down. We have to talk," Dulcy Abbot said.

"I don't have anything to talk about. I just have a job to do, honey," Fargo said as he sat down on the small sofa.

"You can listen," she said and he shrugged.

"Listening never hurt anybody," he said and she sat down beside him and he saw very round breasts push up over the edge of the scoop-necked dress, her skin smoothly soft.

"I know he gave you all kinds of reasons to bring me back but they were all lies," she said.

"Why am I supposed to believe you?" Fargo questioned.

"I think I can convince you. Give me two days. Two days for my life. That's not a lot to ask," she said.

"I guess not," he agreed.

"After all, I am as good as your prisoner now that you've found me," she added and he nodded as he realized he was a little disappointed that the pursuit had ended so abruptly. It was almost anticlimactic and he'd hoped to settle with Brad Ales before catching Dulcy.

"And if I decide to take you back anyway?" he said.

"No fuss. I promise," she said.

"Two days," he grunted and she smiled, a warm,

sweet smile of gratefulness. Dulcy Abbot was a strange combination, he decided.

"I was just heating up some stew. Let's start with supper. Are you hungry?" she asked.

"Yes," he admitted.

"Good. Make yourself comfortable while I get us some supper. They say the way to a man's heart is through his stomach. That's maybe the way to convincing a man, too," she said. He settled back and watched her set two places on the table. She moved with a curvy grace and was most enjoyable to watch, her round breasts pressing against the top of the dress as she turned one way and then another. The meal was good, the stew well spiced, and when they finished he found her watching him with a small smile. "I didn't expect he'd send anyone so handsome after me," Dulcy said. "Though maybe I should have. He's very clever."

"Meaning what exactly?" Fargo queried.

"He knows I've a weakness for handsome men," Dulcy said.

Fargo smiled. "I'll add flattery to your talents," he said.

"No flattery, just being honest. What made you keep on after me? Why didn't you turn back at Kempton?" she asked.

"A trailsman learns to see, not just to look," Fargo said.

"You can bring your bedroll in here," Dulcy said as she cleared away dishes.

"I figured doing that," Fargo said.

"I should have known." Dulcy Abbot smiled and he went outside, unsaddled the Ovaro, and put the horse on a long tether beside the bay gelding. Dulcy was in the other room when he brought his bedroll inside, a small fire in the hearth almost at its end. He had undressed down to his jeans when she came from the other room, a thin, white cotton nightgown that rested against her soft-curved shape, the top open and loose. He saw her eyes move slowly and appreciatively over the muscled symmetry of his torso.

"You want to talk some?" he asked.

"Not about him. I've decided I won't try to convince you that I'm right and he's wrong," she said.

"You giving up?" Fargo asked in surprise.

"No, I'm going to show you I'm a person worth letting go, worth believing in," she said.

"You think maybe you ought to go back? He said he needs your signatures to run the business. You could go back and settle things," Fargo suggested.

"I'm not going to explain any of the things he's told you except to say that he doesn't need me," Dulcy Abbot said, her brown eyes serious.

"That's still making it your word against his. Maybe you can't give me anything more but that's not enough, honey," Fargo said.

She frowned at him for a dozen seconds, her lips pursed. "No, I suppose not," she said finally, turned away, and he watched her go through the curtain into the other room, the thin cotton nightdress clinging to the softness of her very round rear. Fargo finished undressing and slid into his bedroll as the room grew black. Dulcy Abbot's quiet sweetness still surprised him, no fire even in her references to her father. Yet she had cajoled, persuaded, and bought an entire town to lie for her. It just didn't seem to fit. He was still thinking about her when he heard the curtain to the other room part and he sat up as Dulcy entered the room, a lamp turned low in one hand. She set the lamp down and dropped to her knees beside him.

"Been thinking about what you said and decided I can give you more than words," she said, and with a quick motion of both hands, the nightdress came up over her head and fell to the floor.

He held back words as his eyes took in a softly shaped figure, every part of her layered with roundness, breasts full and very round, edging toward flabbiness but still very attractive, each tip dark red against a lighter red circle, over a strong, wide rib cage. Her thighs carried a layer of extra flesh yet held their shapeliness and a neat brown-black triangle seemed inappropriately small. Her body echoed her face, a sweet softness to it that nonetheless carried its own brand of sensuousness. He regarded her speculatively for a long glance.

"I never turn down good whiskey or a warm woman but I want to be fair, honey. What do you expect this is going to mean?" he asked.

"I'm hoping it'll make you want to spend more than two days with me, to want to understand me instead of just rushing me back with you," she said.

He considered her answer. "It might do that," he allowed. "But what if it doesn't?"

A tiny smile touched her face, a mixture of mischievousnus and wantoness. "Then from the looks of you I'll have had two glorious days so it won't be a total loss," Dulcy said.

"Fair enough," he said, reached out, and drew her to him, closing his hands around the soft, round shoulders. Her mouth was against his at once, lips parted, folding around him, her tongue pushing out with instant hunger. She came down onto the bedroll with him, and his hands found her breasts were as fleshily soft as they appeared to be, moving under his touch, the dark red tips erect and firm. She gasped, a low, growling sound as his lips closed around one breast. Her hands slid down his torso, found his erect warmth and closed around him.

"Jeez, yes, oh, Jeez, yes," she cried out as she rolled over, rubbed her little belly against him. She pushed her mound hard against his crotch, pressed, bucked, pressed again, and groaned the low, growling sounds.

"It's been a long time, hasn't it?" he murmured and she nodded almost frantically. She slid her soft, rounded body up and down against his muscled torso and he cupped his hands to the very round, soft rear. Pulling him to her, he felt the full-fleshed thighs fall open, moist warmth closing around his hips.

"Take me, Jeeeeez, take me," Dulcy murmured and her thighs contracted against him as she moved her pubic mound, lifting upward, the lock seeking the key, and when he slid forward into the dark, moist welcome, she screamed in pure ecstasy. She was spacious and eager, moving back and forth with him as he slid deeper and drew back and she was instantly in rhythm with his long, slow thrusts. "Yes, oh yes ... yes," she groaned and drew his face down to the soft, round breasts, pillows of smothering pleasure. He found himself enveloped, drawn into her hungering willingness, into the soft sensuality of her. She was a warm bath of flesh, encompassing, flowing, surrounding, and more of everything than he'd expected. But for all her total immersion in the ecstasy of the flesh, she managed to hold back and prolong each delicious minute until he felt her convex belly rise up and push softly against him. "Now, now, now, oh, Jeeez, now," she groaned in the low, growling sound which rose, not in pitch but only in intensity.

He felt himself carried along with her encompassing ecstasy and heard his own voice join hers in a groan of ultimate release as she clasped his face to her breasts and held him there long after she stopped heaving and her full-fleshed body lay still under his. When he finally drew from her and fell to one side, she rolled with him, still keeping his face against her breasts. "So wonderful," she murmured. "More than I hoped for."

"More than I expected," he said as she drew back and gazed at him. "But we still have to talk tomorrow."

"There are all kinds of ways to talk, some are better than words," she said.

"All right, I'll go along with that," Fargo said. "But sometimes you need words."

"Let's wait and see," Dulcy said. "I want to sleep now."

He nodded his agreement. It had been a long day's ride and tiredness now had a new dimension of sweet relaxation. It would be worth getting to know Dulcy Abbot, he decided. She was plainly a most unusual young woman and she had no hesitation in using whatever approach she felt was best for her goals. That much was very evident as he reflected back at what he had come on to so far. He closed his eyes and slept with her soft roundness against him and when morning came she woke with him, sat up, and stretched contentedly before swinging from the bedroll. "There's a basin by the well outside," she said as she hurried into the other room, soft rear jiggling. He listened to her washing for a few moments before he rose and went outside and she had coffee and biscuits ready when he finished and returned to the cabin. He saw she wore a white shirt under a pair of overalls.

"You look like a farm girl," he told her.

"I've a job helping Satch Miller at his goat farm.

It's hard to raise anything much but cactus out here," she said. "You seem surprised."

"I am," he said. "You've settled in here. You were that sure Kempton would turn away anybody who came after you."

"I was. Guess I made a mistake," she said as she poured him a tin mug of coffee. "I don't suppose you'd let me go to Satch alone. I might run away," she said.

"Bull's eye," Fargo grunted. "I'll be tagging along."

"Then you can help me," she said.

"I didn't say anything about that." He frowned.

"You wouldn't want to sit around and watch me work. It'd be boring," she laughed and his eyes narrowed at her. She had been tracked down, her best laid plans defeated, and yet she was unflustered. He decided admiration had to be mixed with caution. Dulcy was not a young woman to be underestimated. When they finished breakfast he rode with her to a scraggly farm some half-hour away, where he met Satch Miller, a gaunt man, as lean and scraggly as his farm. The goats in the corral seemed a hardy cross of domestic and mountain species and Dulcy handed him a food pail. He muttered under his breath as he followed her into the corrals. "Talk," he growled as he worked beside her, unwilling to let her have things entirely her way.

"Last night was really special," she said.

"Not about that," he snapped. "Why'd you steal two thousand dollars from your pa?"

She was silent for a moment. "I didn't," she said finally.

"You didn't?" he echoed, deciding to trap her.

"That's right," she said crisply.

46

"You tossed plenty of money around Kempton. Where'd that come from?" he speared.

She was silent again for a moment. "The money I took was mine," she said and he swore silently. Rob Abbot had said that she had a small income left to her. He waited but Dulcy said nothing more as she went about her chores. She didn't try to convince him of anything, didn't offer explanations or supply any additional motivation. She simply made flat statements. It was as if she were challenging him to take her at her word. And she was willing to use her body to back up that challenge. "How'd he come to hire you, Fargo?" she asked, interrupting his thoughts.

"I was the right man at the right place," Fargo said as he decided she'd not be the only one to give unsatisfactory answers.

"Lucky for you, unlucky for me," she said with a smile. "So far," she added, a twinkle in her eye as she walked away to refill her pail. Damn her, she had no right to be so likable, he swore inwardly.

"You know Brad Ales? He worked for your pa," Fargo asked.

"No. Why?" Dulcy said.

"I want to find him, too," Fargo answered.

"Why don't you go do that and forget about me?" she smiled brightly.

"Nice try," he muttered and she gave a cheerful shrug.

"Help me get these nannies in the other corral," she said and he went with her as she separated the goats and after the nannies were isolated they were hosed down and then the billy goats brushed. Dulcy worked cheerfully, chattering idly with no attempt to talk about herself. The chores took up the day and when dusk began to gather, he returned to the cabin with her, wondering about her even more. She was a strange one, her behavior, moods, actions, an entwining puzzle. She had offered herself to him, wholly and passionately, and he could assign a half-dozen explanations for that, but she didn't follow through on any level. Nothing about her seemed to fit together right. He had seen the evidence of her cleverness and determination and yet he could see only a warm and willing pleasantness about her now. Unless she was trying to lull him into a state of relaxed acceptance. The thought had crossed his mind a few times and he pondered it again.

If that was her scheme, she was doomed to failure because he was growing more cautious, a long-standing watchword whenever he came onto something that didn't fit right.

"I'll put on a steak I have," she called out cheerily and cut into his thoughts. "You just sit down and relax."

He smiled at the word. "Whatever you say," he answered as she busied herself at the hearth. She brought him a bottle of tequila and a glass and set it down before him. "You're not joining me?" Fargo asked.

"I don't drink, never have. But I thought you might like one," she said.

"Why not?" he said and poured himself some of the tequila as she returned to her cooking. He sniffed it first, then took a sip. She was ready with the steak and some browned potato slices when he finished the tequila, and when the meal was over she led him to the small sofa and sat down beside him.

"I know what you're thinking," she began.

"And what would that be?" he queried.

"That I haven't said anything to convince you to believe in me," she said.

"That's for damn sure," he agreed.

"Last night was really something. I want it again, nothing to get in the way, just you and me enjoying ourselves. It'd mean a lot to me. Tomorrow we'll talk. If what I say doesn't satisfy you, and you don't want to stay on longer with me, I'll go back with you," she said.

He studied her for a moment as the night before circled through his mind, a distinctly pleasant memory. "Fair enough," he said and she rose and took his hand.

"Inside. My bed's softer than your bedroll," she said and led him into the other room, where a candle burned low but afforded enough light for him to see a large bed on a wood frame. She turned to him, released his hand and began to undress, not hurrying, making almost a saloon stripper's way with it, letting the very soft and round breasts spill out one by one, tossing her overalls away with a flourish to reveal the small, fleshy mound of a belly, stretching her fulsome body, and enjoying every moment of revelation. Fargo, feeling himself responding, flung his clothes off and in moments he lay with her atop the bed. Dulcy rolled over on him and began to press and stroke and caress with every part of her body, torso, breasts, thighs, and hands. Once again, she was enveloping, surrounding, and when he finally slid within her throbbing darkness she moaned and groaned in the growly way that was hers and moved with him, suddenly hurrying and he came with her as she exploded around him. "Jeeeeez . . . oh, Jeez," she murmured as she lay against him, panting hard, her round body finally still, content to stay pressed to him.

She stayed that way for perhaps half an hour as he relaxed with her, nuzzling against him, and then he felt her hand creep down along his muscled torso, reach his abdomen, pause, then trace a wispy line across his skin. She moved down further, across his groin, and he felt her fingers close around him, the touch instantly arousing. She rubbed gently, stroked, fondled, and he heard her little cry of pleasure as he rose for her and grew warm and throbbing and suddenly seeking. She was quick to answer, bringing her round little belly over him. She rubbed against his surging flesh, brought her thighs up, and sank over him, warm funnel encompassing his maleness, and she began to move up and down at once, quick, hard movements that she slowed and sped up and slowed again.

Her low, groaning sounds filled the room and she made love to him with a strange combination of intensity and deliberateness, prolonging each sensation, clinging to each moment, pulling him with her as she turned onto her back, then climbing over him again. He found himself echoing her groans of pleasure, surprised but delighted at her abilities and energies. He was more than ready when her groans became a low, growling scream and she slammed herself against him. "Oh, Jeeeeeez, oh, Jeez," Dulcy breathed as she finally fell back beside him, soft breasts heaving. "I need some sleep now," she murmured.

"I'll go along with that. You were something special tonight," he said.

"Inspiration," she said as she turned onto her side and was asleep in moments, her breathing a soft, steady sound. He closed his eyes, fully satiated, and welcomed the restoring powers of sleep. He hadn't any idea of how much time had gone by when he woke, the faint sound brushing his ears, touching his inner senses, which in the way of wild creatures, never completely turned off. He lay motionless and heard the rustle of the curtain that covered the doorway between the two rooms. Turning his head only a fraction, he glimpsed Dulcy disappearing through the curtain.

Still unmoving, he heard her in the other room, the sound of clothes being donned. With the silence of a cougar, he swung from the bed, a little surprised at how silent Dulcy had been not to wake him as she rose. He peered through the partly transparent material of the curtain to see Dulcy, a dress on, slip out of the cabin. He returned to the bed and pulled on his boots and trousers, strapped on his gunbelt, and hurried from the room. He dropped to one knee in the dark doorway of the cabin and peered outside, where a half-moon let him see Dulcy saddling the gelding before she swung onto the horse.

She kept the horse at a walk as she rode from the cabin and he waited to give her enough time to move away through the warm night before he ran to the Ovaro. Disdaining a saddle, he pulled himself onto the horse and set out after Dulcy, using hand and leg pressure to guide the pinto. He picked up the sound of the gelding's hoofbeats as she put the horse into a fast trot and he stayed back, content to follow the sound. Only when a series of sandstone rock formations came into sight did he move in closer, spying her in the passage between the rocks. He kept out of sight, using other passages to draw still closer and then he saw the small house standing alone a few hundred yards on the flatland beyond the rocks. He halted the Ovaro at the edge of the rocks and watched as Dulcy rode to the house, dismounted, and knocked on the door.

The glow of lamplight being turned on followed and

he saw a man answer the door. Dulcy spoke to him but she was too far away for Fargo to catch her words and he waited, his eyes staying on her as she returned to the gelding as the man closed the door. She waited beside the gelding and Fargo frowned as he watched and suddenly the man came from around the rear of the house, astride a short-legged horse. He took off south and Dulcy watched him go for a few moments before she climbed into the saddle and began to ride back the way she had come. Fargo wheeled the Ovaro, cut through narrow passages between the rocks, and put the pinto into a gallop when he reached the other end of the rocks.

He scowled into the darkness as he rode, aware that he knew only one thing. He was going to find out the meaning of the strange, dead-of-night meeting. Dulcy's wild passion had been part of a plan to tire him enough so that he'd stay asleep. That much was obvious now and that added to his anger. He was hardly in a position to feel the cheated lover but he felt he'd surely been taken in, used, duped. Yet, he realized, he could complain about the meaning but not the method. He reached the cabin, tethered the Ovaro exactly where it had been and hurried inside. He flattened himself against the wall inside the second room, just behind the curtained doorway and waited. Dulcy arrived soon after and he heard her pause after she entered the cabin. She peeled off the dress and stepped silently into the bedroom. She stopped, staring at the bed where she'd expected to find him, and he saw her mouth fall open.

"Over here, honey," he said softly and she spun, the soft breasts swaying to one side in unison. Her eyes went to his boots, trousers and gunbelt. "You're not the only one who can pull surprises," he said.

"Besides, you shouldn't go riding alone at this hour of night in this country."

Her eyes narrowed as she pulled her mouth closed and faced his cold gaze. "You followed me," she said.

"I had the feeling I was going to get screwed again, but differently this time," he said and she made no reply. "Start talking. What was that all about?" he said.

"It was just something I had to do, something personal," she answered.

"Try again," he grunted.

"A message I had to deliver, in case you took me back tomorrow," Dulcy said.

"A message to who?" he asked.

"That's not important. It was personal, I told you," she said.

"Not good enough. Try again," Fargo said, his eyes staying hard.

"That's all I'm going to say," she told him.

"I figure it'll be dawn in another hour or so. You send for help?" he questioned.

"No," she said.

"Why don't I believe you?" Fargo growled.

"I didn't send for help," she insisted.

"I guess we'll wait to find out," he said.

"May I put some clothes on?" she asked with a touch of reproof.

"It's a little late for modesty," he said.

"No modesty. I'd just feel better, unless you want to make love again," she said.

"I'll take a raincheck," he said and pulled the curtain back. "You can put that dress back on," he said, nodding to the dress she'd left on the small sofa. She passed him, paused, and he saw defiance in her eyes and then she went on to wriggle into the dress. He pushed her outside with him as he went to his saddle and took the lariat and the big Sharps rifle from it. When he went back into the cabin with her he tied her wrists and ankles and pushed her onto the bed.

"Is this necessary?" she asked acidly.

"Honey, I don't know what's necessary with you," he said as he left her, took the rifle, and went to the lone window in the cabin. The first pink streaks of dawn were touching the distant horizon and he settled down to wait, his lake blue eyes searching the darkness. When the sun finally blanketed the land he continued to wait but nothing moved, no riders approached, cautiously spread out, no tiny figures crouched waiting in the distance. He let the sun move into the noon sky before he drew back from the window just as Dulcy's voice broke the silence.

"Dammit, there's nobody coming. I didn't call for help. I'm thirsty and these ropes are hurting me," she said.

He turned into the bedroom, untied her, and stayed with her as she returned to the other room and drank from a pitcher of water. She turned to him when she put the pitcher down. "I'll go back with you," she said.

"You sure as hell will, honey," he said.

"I mean, I'm ready to go back now. We can start right away," she said and he peered at her.

"First you wanted me to stay and get to know you. Now you're in a hurry to go back," he said.

"I changed my mind. I decided it's best to go back with you," she said.

"Just like that?"

"Just like that," she repeated. She kept her face expressionless as he continued to peer hard at her. Something was wrong, he muttered inwardly. Her about-face was too sudden. Again, she seemed two different people wrapped in one. The thought hung in his mind, suddenly shimmering with new meaning. His eyes were hard as he continued to search her face but his voice was casual.

"Tell me about your pa," he said.

"I won't talk about him. I told you that. Just take me back. I'll pack my things and we can go," she said.

"Tell me what your pa looks like?" Fargo asked. "Is he tall, short, thin, fat? What color is his hair? Does he wear a mustache?"

She couldn't hide the surprise that flooded her face, surprise tinged with sudden alarm. But she was quick, he admitted silently. "You met him. You know what he looks like," she said.

"I want to hear you tell me. Is his hair still dark? Or is it gray? What color are his eyes?" Fargo persisted.

Her lips tightened and he caught the sudden desperation that touched her eyes as she cast about for an answer, afraid to give him a wrong one. "Why all these stupid questions? You know the answers to them," she said belligerently.

"Yes, I do, but you don't," Fargo said and saw her tongue come out to lick at lips suddenly dry. "You don't know what your pa looks like. Now, that's strange, isn't it," Fargo said as he stepped to where a traveling sack lay in a corner of the room. He picked it up and spilled the contents on the floor. Most of it was clothing, ribbons, combs, some jewelry, and powder boxes. But there was a small address book and he picked it up. Opening it, he paused at the line written inside the front cover. "Property of Anita Fox," he read aloud and his eyes bored into her.

"That belongs to a friend of mine," she said but

she looked away and the conviction was gone from her voice.

"Enough bullshit. You're not Dulcy Abbot. You're Anita Fox," he snapped as all the little things that hadn't quite fitted were suddenly fitting. "The truth, dammit."

She glowered back. "I don't have to tell you anything," she said.

"I'm going after that man you met last night. You don't talk and I'm taking you with me," he said and saw the alarm come into her face. "You could end up in a Comanche camp." Her glower faded and she simply looked unhappy. "Christ, what'd she pay you for this kind of loyalty?" he asked in exasperation.

"Enough to send to my sick ma," the young woman answered.

He pulled the harshness from his voice. "Talk to me. She hired you to stand in for her. You did a damn good job of it, Anita. You're paid up," he said. He took her arm and led her to the sofa. She sat down and shrugged in defeat.

"She found me in a crummy little town and hired me, paid me more than I'd ever seen at one time," the young woman said. "She told me she was running away from her pa and that's all I needed to know about that."

"But she had to tell you about Kempton," Fargo said and Anita Fox nodded.

"She told me that it would probably end there and how she'd arranged everything. But she wasn't going to take chances. She wanted to be ready in case someone somehow didn't believe what she'd set up in Kempton. It turned out she was right to hire me. You weren't fooled. You showed up here," Anita Fox said.

"And you did your job. You tried to keep me here

and give up the chase. When that blew up in your face you went into part two of her instructions, right?" Fargo said and Anita nodded glumly.

"I was to ask you to take me back," she said.

"If I had that would have bought her another week, maybe two," Fargo said. "The man you met last night, he was part of her plan, too, wasn't he?"

"Yes. He was a messenger. She paid him to stay here and wait. If anyone got past Kempton I was to tell him," Anita said.

"You know where he went?"

"No. He had his orders but he never told me. That's the truth, Fargo," she said and her hand reached out to cover his. "I know I lied to you and you're not much for believing me but I was doing my job. I'm not lying to you now and those times we had together, they weren't lies, either."

"Didn't think they were," he said and she questioned with a quick glance. "I knew you couldn't be that good a liar," he smiled and she shrugged. There was a sudden, rueful shyness to her. He really had nothing against the young woman. She had never properly fit the image he'd built in his mind of Dulcy Abbot, he reminded himself. Dulcy Abbot would never have her kind of softness, outside or inside. "What are you going to do now, Anita?" he asked.

"Go north, visit my ma in Kansas. There's a stage stops by here every two weeks. They know me here as Dulcy Abbot. I can't suddenly say I'm not and I don't fancy staying here and living a lie," she said. "You're going on after her, aren't you?"

"That's right. I'll start with the tracks of that messenger," Fargo said. "Tell me one more thing. Dulcy put out an image of herself in Kempton as being sweet and warm and she had you carry that out here. What did you think of her?"

"She was real nice to me. Very patient. She took her time coaching me in everything, even how to turn off questions about her pa," Anita said. "It was easy to see that she was real smart." Fargo gave a wry grunt. That fact was becoming crystal clear. "Fact is, the only time I ever saw her seem a little hard was when she mentioned her pa," Anita added.

"What'd she tell you about him? She tell you why she was running away?" Fargo queried.

"No, and she never really said anything about him, only her face would change when she used his name," Anita said.

"Thanks," Fargo said. "Guess I'll be going on now."

Anita stepped forward, brought her lips up to his, warm echoes as she clung for a moment. "Thanks for not hating me," she said. "I wish it could've worked out so we spent more time together. I'll be remembering you."

"Same here," he said. He kissed her again and then he was outside, saddling the Ovaro. She stayed in the house as he rode away. He put the horse into a fast canter as he rode to the shack and picked up the line of tracks moving south. He uttered a grunt of satisfaction. The man's horse had a jagged piece missing on the right forefoot shoe. The trail would be easy to pick out. It was time he had a break in the chase for Dulcy Abbot, he muttered to himself as he sent the pinto south.

4

The rider had set a hard pace and Fargo followed until night fell. He found a spot alongside a pinnacle rock and bedded down. He ate some cold jerky he had in his saddlebag and found himself thinking about Dulcy Abbot. He was growing more impressed with her each day. Everything she had done had been designed to buy her time. She had planned ingeniously, with attention to detail, setting up precautions and back-up procedures. Was she also the sweet, warm person everyone said she was? Or was that just another part of the detailed, clever planning? He looked forward to finding that out perhaps more than bringing her back, he realized as he drew sleep around himself.

The night was quiet, interrupted only by the distant howls of the red wolf, and he woke with the hot morning sun. He picked up the trail again, pausing only to breakfast on the pulp of the prickly pear, using his double-edged throwing knife to carve out the rich interior. As he followed the tracks, the terrain changed character and grew less arid with patches of black walnut and water oak along with hackberry and chinquapin oak. The land became dotted with low hills as well as sandstone formations and he swept the terrain with long, piercing glances as he rode. The day slid into the afternoon when he spotted the line of unshod hoofprints and he swung from the saddle, letting his fingers move across the tracks. They were fresh, the edges firm and slightly moist, not more than a half-hour old, he grimaced.

When he rode on he slowed the pinto almost to a walk and he had crested a low hill when he swung behind a pair of hackberry and halted. Below him the line of horsemen had made a circle and were moving back up the hill toward him. No Comanche, he grunted silently. Mescalero Apache, perhaps not as stealthy as the Comanche, perhaps not quite as good trackers, but every bit as fierce and, some said, crueler. He counted seven as he unholstered his sixgun, not the kind of odds to give the Mescalero. He scanned the land through the hackberry as he sought the best way to make a run for it if they found him.

But the mostly near-naked riders halted halfway up the low hill, spaced apart, and turned their ponies to face down to the flatland. They settled down, waiting, and Fargo cursed under his breath. He had no choice but to wait and lose more precious time tracing Dulcy's messenger. But he'd choose trying to run only if he had to and he dropped the Colt back in its holster to wait in frustration as the sun slid its way toward the horizon. He wondered what they waited for when the answer came into sight—a half-dozen white-tailed deer moving along the flatland. Using sign commands, the Mescalero exploded into action, separating as they raced their ponies downhill. The deer started to bound one way, then shifted as they glimpsed two of the riders coming in from the other side. They whirled, leaping in long bounds, the moment's confusion costing them fatal seconds.

Fargo saw three of the Apache close in on one

frightened doe. Using their short bows they sent a volley of arrows into her. The deer ran for another dozen yards before dropping and the other hunters returned to the spot. They had brought down only one but that was enough, and using lengths of rawhide, they trussed the animal's legs and dragged it behind them as they rode away. Fargo let a sigh of relief escape him and waited till they were out of sight before he moved from the hackberry and began to follow the hoofprints again. The man had continued almost straight south and once again Fargo pursued until night fell. He bedded down in a cluster of black walnut and when the new day dawned he put the pinto into a fast canter to make up for time lost.

By midafternoon he had trailed the tracks with but one stop to let the Ovaro rest and he saw the buildings of a town come into sight. The tracks led directly to the town and Fargo felt the excitement rising inside him. With the original head start he had, and the delays that followed, the rider had reached the town two days ago, Fargo estimated. That meant Dulcy could well still be here. He put the pinto into a fast trot and rode into town past a weathered sign that read LONG-LEY. It was a shabby place, every building in need of paint, many with sagging roofs, but he saw a good number of Owensboro farm wagons lining the main street and he took note of a building marked LONGLEY BANK.

The tracks he followed were quickly obliterated in the dirt of the street by wheel tracks and the hoof-prints of other horses and he drew up before a worn building with a BED AND BOARD sign outside.

A portly man in shirtsleeves lounged in the doorway and Fargo called to him from the saddle. "You clerk here, mister?" he asked and the man nodded. "I'm looking for a young woman named Dulcy Abbot. She boarding here by any chance?" Fargo said and saw the man's eyes widen as he straightened up.

"You better see the mayor," the man said. "At the end of the street."

"You've a mayor in this town?" Fargo frowned in surprise.

"End of the street," the man said tersely and Fargo moved on, rode slowly past a flat-roofed building simply marked SALOON, and reached a small narrow structure that seemed mostly a tall window. He dismounted and entered the building to see a man behind a small desk, dark-haired, pushing forty or so years, Fargo guessed, wearing a four-in-hand with a ruffled shirt.

"This the mayor's office?" Fargo asked.

"You come for the funeral?" the man returned. "Tomorrow morning."

"Not again. She wouldn't try pulling the same act twice," Fargo groaned aloud.

"I beg your pardon?" the man said.

"The funeral. Who's is it?" Fargo queried.

"The mayor's funeral. I'm acting mayor, Tom Tilson," the man said and frowned up at the big man in front of him. "You're not here for the funeral?"

"I'm here looking for a young woman, Dulcy Abbot. Don't bother telling me she's sweet and wonderful. I've heard all that," Fargo said.

"The bitch, there's nothing sweet and wonderful about her. She's why we're having a funeral for the mayor," Tilson said. Fargo felt his brow lift as something close to shock swept through him.

"Dulcy Abbot? Brown hair, brown eyes, tall?" he questioned.

"That's right. The goddamn bitch killed the mayor, damn near killed Sheriff Gibbs, too, only the doc managed to pull him through. Shot the both of them, the rotten, stinking little bitch," Tom Tilson said.

Fargo stared at Tilson. This was a very different Dulcy Abbot from the one he'd been hearing about and he still wrestled with the shock of it. "When did all this happen?" he asked.

"Night before last," Tilson answered. Fargo repeated the answer inside himself. Two nights ago. The messenger might have reached Dulcy before, but then he might not have. Fargo swore silently.

"You know why she shot your mayor and the sheriff?" he asked.

"No. I just know she asked to meet them and when they went to see her she shot them," Tilson said.

Fargo frowned at the answer. It was a total departure from anything Dulcy had done this far, but then nothing about Dulcy seemed to fit. She had a good head start and she'd made very clever plans for every contingency, even to a special courier on standby. Why hadn't she kept her lead? Why hadn't she kept going? Why had she spent three weeks in this shabby little town. One more strange twist but this one was a mixed blessing. He was a lot closer to Dulcy now than he'd expected to be but he'd left the other two towns with leads to follow. This time he had no idea which way she had gone. Unless, and he paused at the thought, the messenger hadn't met with her. In that case, if he was still going on, his tracks could be picked up again. Fargo turned and strode from the narrow office. "Sorry about the mayor," he called back as he left and climbed onto the Ovaro.

He rode from the town, aware there was not too much left of the day, and when he was beyond the town he peered at the tracks that led south, wagon wheel tracks and a number of hoofprints. He walked the horse slowly, scanning the ground for the unmistakable nicked right forefoot shoe. He saw a number of wheel tracks turn off the main road and some prints go their own way, but he kept on southward as the trails thinned out and grew easier to distinguish. But the print with the nicked hoof didn't appear and when dusk turned into night, he swung back and returned to the town. He turned the possibilities in his mind as he rode. There weren't that many. The courier met with Dulcy, delivered his message, and turned back. Or Dulcy had already left and he'd never delivered his message. He wouldn't have gone on then, either.

Perhaps he had turned back. But perhaps he was still in town. Fargo embraced the thought at once. Dulcy's courier might provide a lead. It was a chance he couldn't pass up and as night fell he rode into town, drew up in front of the saloon, and tethered the Ovaro. His gaze traveled along the two horizontal tethering bars as he went into the saloon and ordered a bourbon at the bar. He drank slowly, making seemingly casual talk with the bartender as he let the saloon fill up. It was a scruffy place, a lot of sawdust and a few tables, no saloon girls, and most of the customers came to drink and tell tall stories.

"Been looking for three friends of mine. One has a scar on his chin. They stop by here?" he asked the bartender.

"Matter of fact they did, few days back. I remember the one with the scar," the bartender said and Fargo grunted inwardly. The trip would not be a total loss.

"They mention where they were heading?" he asked as he ordered another bourbon.

"I heard one talk about San Antonio," the bartender said. "But I told them about Sam Walleston up near Lampasas. He's hiring hands for a cattle drive, told them they could pick up some extra money along the way."

"What'd they say?" Fargo asked, excitement gathering inside him.

"The one with the scar said they'd go see Sam. I guess he might have another day or so of hiring in case you're interested," the man said.

"Much obliged," Fargo said and cloaked the grim satisfaction within himself. It seemed as if the personal part of his pursuit might be rewarded. He brought his eyes back to the bar and let his gaze move across the drinkers and the tables with a long, slow sweep. No one new had entered for at least a half-hour. The men at the bar and the tables were determinedly drinking, some in groups of three or four, some alone. He scanned the loners again even as he knew it was fruitless to try and make guesses. Paying for the last bourbon, he strolled from the saloon to pause outside. The line of tethered horses had grown considerably longer and he started at the end nearest him, a tall light-brown gelding the first horse. He lifted the animal's right foreleg and peered at the hoof, running one finger along the edge of the horseshoe, unwilling to trust only his eyes in the darkness. Its horseshoe bore no nicked place and he went on to the next horse.

Slowly and carefully, he worked his way down the line of horses, examining each right forefoot. He had to stop and drop to the ground as two men followed by a third came from the saloon and swung onto their horses. But they rode mounts he had already checked and when they rode away he returned to his task. He was nearing the last of the horses and beginning to feel discouraged when his finger moving along the edge of a horseshoe came to a sudden stop, the V-shaped nick unmistakable. He put the horse's foot down, saw that the animal was a sturdy brown mare, and he quickly walked to the Ovaro and climbed into the saddle. He moved to the other side of the street facing the saloon and backed against an old shed, where he waited, watching each figure who came from the saloon.

There were but a half-dozen horses left when the lone figure came out and went to the brown mare. Fargo felt himself stiffen as he watched the man climb onto the horse and ride unhurriedly down the dark main street of town. Fargo stayed back as he followed the rider from town and up the side of a low rise, where the man finally halted and slid from his horse. Halting under a wide hawthorn, Fargo dismounted as he watched the man set out his bedroll and prepare for the night. He waited until the man took off his shirt and gunbelt before he stepped forward, one hand resting on the butt of the Colt in its holster.

"Don't get too comfortable, friend," he said and the man whirled in surprise. The courier started to bend his knees and reach for the holster on the ground. "Don't even think of it," Fargo said and the man straightened up.

"All I've got is a few dollars. Take 'em," the man said.

"Where's Dulcy Abbot?" Fargo questioned and the man's eyes widened.

"Who are you?" the man asked.

"I'm the one who's come after her," Fargo said. "Where is she?"

"Gone," the man said.

"I know that. But you're still here. You waiting for her to come back to meet you?" Fargo questioned.

"No. I just decided to stay on a few days," the man said.

"Did you meet with her? Did you deliver the message from the girl in Blackwood?" Fargo asked and the man nodded. "What'd she say?" Fargo pressed.

"She was real mad. Upset, too," the courier said.

"What happened then?"

"She paid me what I had coming and that was it. Next day I heard she shot the mayor and the sheriff and took off."

"You know where?"

"No," the man said.

"She didn't say anything to you?" Fargo questioned "No more instructions?"

"No, nothing," the courier said and Fargo wondered if a little pressure might bring different answers. He pulled the Colt out and pushed the barrel into the man's cheekbone.

"I get very angry if people lie to me," he said and watched the fear come into the man's face.

"I'm not lying. She paid me to wait and take a message to her if it came up. She didn't tell me anything more. I'd tell you if I knew anything. Jesus, I don't owe her anything. It was a job," the courier said.

Fargo pulled the gun away, convinced the man was telling the truth, and he reached down and picked up the gunbelt. "I'll put this under that hawthorn. Don't try coming after me," he warned.

"No, sir. You can count on that," the man said. Fargo grunted, strode to the Ovaro, and dropped the gunbelt on the ground as he swung into the saddle. He rode away at a fast trot and kept riding for a mile or so before he bedded down beneath a small stand of shagbark hickory. He still had no idea why Dulcy had waited three weeks in Longley or why she had shot the mayor and the sheriff. But he was strangely not surprised. It was somehow more in character with the woman who had planned so thoroughly and cleverly than the warm, sweet image she had fostered. But Dulcy would take a back seat in the morning, he promised himself as he fell into sleep.

5

Sam Walleston's place turned out to be further north than he'd expected but he found the sprawling layout with corrals filled with cattle consisting of mostly longhorns with a few whiteface thrown in. He took in the four bunkhouses to one side as he rode up to a large structure with the word OFFICE painted on it. A medium-built man with a slight paunch and too much fat around his jowls came out to greet him and shifted a mostly chewed cigar from one side of his mouth to the other. He held a large notepad in one hand.

"If you're looking for work we stopped hiring yesterday," he said.

"I'm looking for a man name of Brad Ales. You hire him on? He's got two friends with him," Fargo said.

Sam Walleston ruffled through the pages of his notepad. "Yes, Brad Ales, Johnson, and Olmey, hired 'em at the same time," he said. "You a friend of Ales'?"

"We rode together," Fargo said.

"They're in bunkhouse 4, the last one," the man said. "Unless they went to town. Some of the men did. We'll be starting come morning."

"Much obliged. I'll just be paying a short visit," Fargo said as he headed the horse toward the bunkhouse. He made a wide circle and came up to the house from the back side, dismounted, and moved to the lone window on foot. He glimpsed a half-dozen saddled horses on a loose rope tether near the other end of the bunkhouse. Peering through the dirt glass of the window, he saw Olmey first, lounging on one of six bunks in the structure. He found Johnson next, seated on another of the bunks. They seemed to be the only ones in the house and he was scanning the room again when he heard the curse of surprise.

"Shit," the voice said and he whirled to see Brad Ales on a horse, some dozen yards away. He had come up and had recognized the Ovaro at once. Fargo saw he already had his sixgun drawn and he dived, hit the ground, and rolled as a volley of bullets slammed into the bunkhouse wall. He kept rolling and flung himself around the corner of the building as more bullets grazed his heels. Ales spurred the horse forward to follow but the split-second had been enough time for Fargo to draw his Colt and he fired as Ales started to come around the building.

Ales drew back at once and Fargo heard Olmey and Johnson shouting as they ran from the bunkhouse. "We're gettin' out of here," Ales shouted and Fargo dropped to one knee as he peered around the building to see Ales racing away and Johnson and Olmey climbing onto their horses. He also saw Sam Walleston appear and a dozen more figures emerge from the other bunkhouses, surprise and confusion on their faces. Ales, with Johnson and Olmey chasing after him, headed for a long line of Spanish oak. They didn't want questions anymore than he did but for different reasons. Fargo ran to the Ovaro, vaulted into the saddle and had the horse at a gallop in seconds as he raced after the fleeing trio. Sam Walleston and the others looked on, faces still wreathed in surprise. But Walleston barked no orders to give chase. He was understandably not inclined to interfere in a private shootout.

Ales and the other two men disappeared into the Spanish oak and Fargo followed, the Colt in his hand as he entered the trees. They ran in a long line but with no depth and Fargo heard the three riders racing from the other side. He stayed after them and saw the rise of rocky hills, glimpsed Brad Ales slowing to glance back from atop a granite ledge as Johnson and Olmey caught up to him. Ales saw him moving fast across an open space and up the passageway, wheeled his horse and moved deeper into the rocks. Fargo steered the pinto up the short passage, slowed to listen, and heard the three fleeing horses still moving through the rock-lined hills. He chose a pass through the stone walls that took him east of the fleeing trio but ran in an almost straight line, and he let the Ovaro charge upward at a full gallop.

He reached the top and turned to see Ales and the other two men just threading their way through a narrow crevice to the top of the hill less than twenty yards away. He holstered the Colt and drew the big Sharps rifle from its saddle holster, lifted the gun to his shoulder, and moved the pinto forward with knee pressure. The trio paused to glance back, listening to see where their pursuer was along the narrow passageway. Fargo, a few feet higher, moved another six yards closer before he raised his voice. "Stay where you are and drop your guns," he called out. The three men turned in their saddles to look up at him for an instant and then kicked their horses in the ribs and raced for cover, each in a different direction. Ales, closest to a round rock, disappeared first and Fargo swung the rifle to his right, Olmey in his sights. "Stop, dammit," he shouted again but Olmey was about to vanish behind another rock. Fargo fired and Olmey's body jerked as he flew from the saddle and the horse went on behind the rock.

Fargo watched the man hit against the rock and slide down, leaving a red smear on the gray granite. "Stupid ass," Fargo muttered as he leaped from the Ovaro and in a crouch ran toward the place where Johnson and Brad Ales had taken cover. He dropped behind a rock with a jagged top and listened. Brad Ales was to his right someplace and Johnson to his left, both behind a series of round rocks and neither far from the other. "Nobody else has to get shot," Fargo called out. "Just put your hands up and come out."

"Like hell," Johnson shouted back.

"Shut up, you goddamn fool," Ales swore and Fargo smiled.

"Thank you," he said and immediately heard Ales scrambling to another spot behind the rocks. Fargo brought the rifle back to the second round boulder behind which Johnson's voice had sounded. There was no sound of movement. Johnson was staying where he was and Fargo started to crawl along the jagged rock where he was positioned, moving to the left, pausing when he reached the end of it. Then, on steps silent as a mountain lion's, he left the shelter of the rock and crossed to the other side of the narrow passage. He halted, listened, and began to make his way upward along a slanting side of sandstone, once again moving noiselessly. He was on his stomach when he reached the top, inching his way upward until he could peer over the edge. Johnson was crouched a few feet

72

below and a dozen yards away, sixgun in hand, head bent forward, listening.

Fargo's glance went to the narrow passageway beyond Johnson that led upward. Brad Ales was hiding there and Fargo rose to his feet as Johnson stayed in place, still listening intently. Fargo aimed the big Sharps but not at Johnson. Instead, he pointed the rifle where the passageway opened just beyond Johnson's crouched form. "Don't move, Johnson. I've got you covered," he called out and, from the corner of his eye, he saw the man stiffen but stay immobilized. Split-seconds later Brad Ales appeared in his gunsight as he stepped from the passage, sixgun in hand as he expected to find his target aiming at Johnson. Fargo's finger tightened on the trigger as Brad Ales's eyes widened for an instant and the sound of the rifle reverberated amid the rocks.

"Ow, Jesus," Ales screamed as his right kneecap shattered, his own shot going wild. He fell forward, losing his gun and Fargo caught the movement below and to his right. Johnson was turning onto his side as he brought his pistol up to fire. Once again the big Sharps erupted and when the echoes stopped bouncing among the rocks, Johnson lay lifeless and the only sound was Ales's pain-filled curses. Fargo stepped down to where Brad Ales lay with one leg drawn up.

"Stupid fools, all of you," Fargo bit out.

"Jesus, my knee ... oh God," Ales cried out.

"Where's the money you stole from me?" Fargo demanded.

"In my pouch, on the saddle," the man answered. Fargo stepped to the horse, fished inside the leather pouch, and drew out a roll of bills he guessed were less than half what they once had been. "I need a doc, real bad," Ales whimpered.

"Try Longley," Fargo said as he stuffed the bills into his pocket.

"You have to help me get there," Ales said.

"I don't have to help you find shit," Fargo rasped. "This'll teach you to hire people and then dry-gulch them."

Brad Ales managed a resentful glare through his pain. "I never figured you'd come after me."

"Why not? I don't take kindly to being robbed," Fargo said.

"I figured you'd be chasing after the damn girl," Ales said.

The frown dug into Fargo's brow at once as he stared at the man. "How do you know about that?" he queried.

"Hell, Abbot set it up," Ales said and Fargo felt the frown dig deeper.

"Try that again," he said.

"Abbot, he's behind everything. He had me hire you and then dry-gulch you," Ales said.

"Why?" Fargo snapped.

"You were the only one who could track down the girl but he was afraid it wasn't the kind of job you'd take unless you were broke enough and mad enough. So he set that up to happen."

Fargo continued to frown down at Brad Ales as a swirl of little things suddenly took on new dimensions. It explained why Ales had left him alive and why he'd waited to the very last day of the drive to do his dry-gulching. It also explained why Rob Abbot just happened to have a job for him to make up what he had lost. Coincidence was suddenly prearranged and he recalled how Abbot had insisted he forget about Ales and concentrate solely on finding Dulcy. "I'll be damned," he breathed. Dulcy wasn't the only one who concocted cleverly planned schemes. Perhaps it ran in the family, he sniffed, not without anger. He'd have some settling to do with Rob Abbot when he returned, with or without Dulcy. Brad Ales moaned again and Fargo brought his attention back to the man.

"Get me back to Longley," Ales said.

"I'll help you onto your horse. You're on your own from there," Fargo rasped.

"I'll need help," Ales complained.

"Take it or leave it," Fargo snapped and when Ales fell silent he walked to the man's horse, brought the steed over and half lifted, half swung Ales into the saddle. The man cried out in pain but clung to the saddle horn with both hands and sent the horse at a slow walk down the rock-lined passage. Fargo waited till Ales was out of sight before making his own way from the rocks and as night descended he bedded down under the line of Spanish oak.

He felt as though he were looking at a picture that remained the same except that new colors had been painted in. He'd put aside the resentment that had formed inside him, the feeling of having been taken, to concentrate on the mechanics of finding Dulcy Abbot. He had damn little to go on now, but he had to start with the basics. She had met with the messenger, then shot the mayor and the sheriff and fled. He'd try to pick up a trail, a lone rider, and hope he had picked up the right one. One thing was certain. He'd be using every bit of experience and instinct he had gathered over the years. But then, he reminded himself, he had found needles in haystacks before.

In the morning he made his way back to the outskirts of Longley, taking a detour around Sam Walleston's herd of cattle as they moved northeast. Halting outside the town, he scanned the ground, his practiced eyes moving across the profusion of hoofprints and wagon wheel tracks. There were far too many to sort out and he concentrated on those leaving town as he slowly followed along the road that led south. He swore silently as he rode. Too many single riders, too many prints. But he followed with dogged persistence, pausing at each set of hoofprints that turned off before going on again. The prints finally thinned out and became the tracks of four single riders. He halted finally and dismounted and dropped to one knee to let his hands move across the prints.

One set was still moist just below the edges, not more than a day old, and he eliminated that rider. But the other three sets of prints had all begun to dry out. They could all be two to three days old, he estimated as he rose and returned to the saddle. He continued to follow the three sets of prints until they began to separate, one turning left, the other going off at a right angle, and the third staying straight. He halted the pinto again and peered at the hoofprints of the three horses for a long minute, intently examining each set until, with a grim snort, he decided to follow the prints that went on straight south. They were a fraction less deep than the other two sets. Either they were made by a lighter horse or a horse with a lighter rider. He desperately hoped it was the latter as he put the Ovaro into a fast trot.

There was little left of the road when the hoofprints turned north and crossed a series of low hillocks to finally halt at a spot bordered by scraggly hawthorns and a wide boulder. He frowned down at the hoofprints only a half-dozen feet away, horses too tightly bunched together for him to count numbers. Raising his eyes, he saw the prints of the lone rider go on south and the other horses also move away in a south-west direction. They stayed pretty much together, but as they moved on they separated enough for him to hazard a count. Four riders, he estimated, perhaps six. They moved into the scraggly hawthorn that dotted the low hills and he continued after the lone rider. A meeting prearranged? Or a chance encounter with a few greetings exchanged and everyone going their way?

That appeared to be the most likely explanation and he stayed after the lone rider, all too aware he might well be following a very wrong trail. But he refused to speculate about that possibility. The question rode with him nonetheless, not unlike a toothache, nagging, irritating. But he'd find the answer soon enough as he saw that he was making good time. At each pause when he dismounted to run his hands across the hoof-prints he found they were growing less dry, and by the time dusk descended he guessed the rider was not more than half a day ahead. He headed down under a hackberry and welcomed sleep.

In the morning he took up the trail again and it was near noon under a burning sun when he came to a wide but very shallow stream. He halted and read the ground as other men read a book. The rider had dis-mounted here to let the horse drink from the stream. Because of the water, the ground was less dry than the Texas soil he'd been traveling across and a carpet of Resurrection moss spread itself outward from the edge of the stream. His eyes halted at a square area a few yards from the stream. The moss had been flat-tened, a blanket spread out and slept upon. Fargo dis-mounted and knelt on one knee beside the area, pressing his hand down over the moss. It hadn't dried out yet. The rider had bedded down here during the night. He rose, took a few steps forward and saw the footprints on the edge of the stream, the imprints just beginning to dry out.

His quarry had risen, washed in the stream, and ridden on, only a few hours ago and Fargo returned to the Ovaro as excitement pulled at him. He put the horse into a fast canter as he followed the hoofprints that led on across land that grew thicker with small hillocks and somewhat thin-stemmed black walnut. The trees grew denser along one side and a line of low rock formations rose opposite them. The hoofprints marked a line in between as they led the way over a low rise. He had just followed their trail over the crest when he saw the dark bay horse a few hundred yards below, standing alone, untethered, but no one near it.

Slowing the Ovaro to a walk, Fargo drew the Colt as he moved down the other side of the rise, his eyes sweeping the rocks and the trees as he neared the horse. He had just reached the animal when the figure stepped from the trees. Automatically, the Colt rose in his hand but his eyes grew narrow and the surge of satisfaction swept through him. He stared at a tall, lean figure wearing riding britches and a white shirt and he took in the brown hair, worn almost shoulder length. The brown eyes came next, but no softness to these. Instead, a dark sharpness and a deep glitter, and he swept the figure again and saw a narrow waist and longish breasts that pushed the white shirt out without effort. "Dulcy Abbot," he said softly.

Her brown eyes appraised him and she let fine-lined lips purse in thought, the sun glinting on high cheekbones and a straight nose, a taut face, handsome rather than pretty, an angular beauty in it. "You're something special," she said. "You do a mean job of trailing."

"You do a mean job of covering a trail," Fargo said.

"Not mean enough, it seems," she sniffed.

"It would have been for most people. I'm not most people," he said as he holstered the revolver.

"That's pretty obvious. Who are you?" she asked.

"Name's Skye Fargo. Some call me the Trailsman," he said.

She gave a little snorting sound. "That figures. He'd hire the best," she said and ran one hand through her thick, deep brown hair and then tossed her head defiantly and her hair shook from side to side.

"I'll ask the questions now," Fargo said.

"No time for questions, señor," the voice interrupted and Fargo's hand dropped to the Colt. "Pull the gun and you are a dead man," the voice said. Fargo turned in the saddle to peer at the rocks and saw the five horsemen, all holding sixguns aimed at him as they moved their horses into the open. He swept them with a single glance, roving *banditos* from south of the border, wide-faced, olive-skinned, mustached, all but two wearing cartridge belts crisscrossing their chests. He hesitated but decided that numbers and distance made the odds unattractive and he dropped his hand to his side. He turned back to Dulcy.

"The ones you met in the hills?" he asked and she nodded. "You hire them then?" he questioned.

"No. I hired them some time ago to do some scouting for me," she said and he sat quietly in the saddle as one of the men moved up and took the Colt from its holster.

"A fine gun, this, señor," the man said. "Aquena will enjoy this gun."

Fargo swore silently at himself. Once again, he had underestimated Dulcy Brown. Once again she had prepared. "But they came in handy for some more work," he said to Dulcy, his voice hard.

"I'm sorry about this but it's my life on the line," she said.

"Is it?" he snorted. "Or do you just want a reason to live with yourself?"

The brown eyes grew deeper. "I want to live. That means I don't go back until I'm ready and I can't have someone trying to bring me back. I'm sorry but this is the way it has to be."

"You'll forgive me if I'm less than grateful," Fargo grunted.

She turned to the man who'd called himself Aquena. "You've your orders," she said, then strode to her horse and rode away without a backward glance. Four of the *banditos* surrounded Fargo and his wrists were bound in front of him so he could grip the saddle horn. With Aquena leading, they began the climb higher into the hills, winding through narrow passages, the terrain becoming steeper and strewn with boulders and jagged stone slabs.

"She is some *mujer*, that one," Aquena chortled and the others joined him in shouts of agreement. He cast a glance back at Fargo. "You don't agree, amigo?" he said.

"I agree," Fargo said, his eyes peering down into the narrow chasms they skirted.

"She ask do we have a place to keep you for a month. We say yes and she pay us, *mucho dinero*," Aquena went on and followed with a harsh laugh.

"But you don't aim to do that, do you?" Fargo said.

The man flashed a gold-toothed smile. "A month is such a long time to sit around watching somebody. We have better ideas," he said.

"I'll bet you do," Fargo said as he saw the rock-lined chasms growing deeper. He knew he had only a few minutes left before Aquena would find the spot he wanted, shoot him, and throw his body over one of the cliffsides. But the passage had grown narrower and it became impossible for his captors to keep a rider on each side of him. One had to fall back, leaving Aquena and one other directly in front of him, two behind and only one alongside him. Fargo, his mouth growing tight, gathered every muscle in his body, pressed down onto the Ovaro's stirrups, and cast another glance over the edge of the chasm. The side was steep, yet not completely straight, rocks and scrub brush jutting out. But it was an awfully long way to the bottom, he realized. Perhaps it would be suicide, yet to delay longer meant only certain death. It was hardly much of a choice yet it was the only one he had left.

Half rising, he catapulted himself from the Ovaro, twisting his body as he did, and flung himself sideways. He felt his shoulder hit the top edge of the passageway as he plunged over the side and he heard the startled shouts of the *banditos*, and then he was falling, hurtling downward. His bound wrists held together, he kept his arms pressed against his sides as he fell, bouncing off one jutting piece of rock, then another, pain shooting through him each time. He heard the sound of the bullets as the men fired down at his plunging body. A jutting piece of mountain scrub brush hit against him, turning him onto his side and he rolled for some fifty feet before a small ledge of rock hit against his back and spun him almost head down and he heard his own cry of pain.

The shots were still popping sounds but they were almost obliterated by the pain in his body as he fell, rolled, turned, and smashed against one protrusion and then another and kept falling. Bullets still slammed into the rocks but they were off target and he managed to glimpse the bottom of the chasm almost in front of him. A rounded boulder loomed up, and with his last bit of strength he half turned his pain-wracked body so that he struck against the round side of the rock. It let him slide against it and acted as a buffer to his body slamming full force into the bottom of the chasm. But he felt consciousness leaving him as he hit bottom and he lay still, facedown, dimly aware of three bullets pinging against the rocks nearby before the world disappeared.

He had no idea how long he lay unconscious when his eyelids fluttered and he began a slow return to awareness. Yet, with the instinctual demand for survival, he knew he had to lay still and he did so, letting full consciousness slowly envelope him. Even unmoving, he was aware of the pain that consumed every part of his body, but he was alive and he offered a silent cry of gratitude. He lay still, his ears straining, but there was no sound, no voices from above, no more shots, and finally he slowly turned on his side and cried out with the pain of it. He could see up the side of the chasm to the top. They had gone, assumed he was dead either from the fall or their bullets. *Wrong, you bastards,* he hissed and his lips pulled back in a grimace of triumph. Despite the pain of every rock he struck, he had forced himself to keep his body limp, letting himself be thrown and turned and twisted without the resistance that would certainly have shattered bone and muscle.

Slowly crying out in pain again, he sat up and rested. He gingerly flexed arm and leg muscles and saw that nothing was broken. Then, staring at the ground, he saw that after bouncing from the last round boulder, luck had come to his aid once more. He had landed on a large, thick growth of Halberd Fern that had spelled the difference between broken bones and bruises. His wrists were still bound together but the fall had loosened the ropes a little. Yet not enough for him to work free and he lay on his side, drew his right leg up until he could reach the calf holster with the razor sharp double-edged Arkansas toothpick. He drew the knife from the holster, turned it in his fingers, and began to cut against the wrist ropes. They had loosened enough to allow him some play and his fingers didn't cramp as quickly as they might have. Yet he had to pause often enough and a half-hour had passed before he cut through the ropes and fell back to rest for a moment, stretching his fingers as he did.

He rose, finally, put the knife back into its calf-holster, and let his gaze travel upward along the wall of rock. It was steep but there were crevices, he saw, and protrusions of stone and growths of tough brush that grew almost directly out from between the rock. Drawing a deep breath and pushing aside the pain, he began to climb and quickly found that every reach and pull was made of agony. He had to pause after almost each one at first. Clinging with his fingers to the horizontal crevices in the rock, he found a place to push with his toes. But he continued again each time, sometimes crying out with the pain of his bruised and stretched muscles.

He was halfway up the steep side when he rested on a narrow ledge for almost fifteen minutes before forcing his protesting muscles to climb again. He was aware that not only did pain make him move with agonizing slowness but one slip and he'd plunge downward and this time there'd be little chance he'd survive. But the hot sun that would normally add to his miseries was a blessing, this time warming strained muscles and tendons. Yet as he slowly continued to pull himself upward he realized he was losing strength and he felt the terrible weakness pull at his body. Muscles were at the end of their strength, the limitations of the flesh crying out. He clung for a long minute, arched his neck backward, and looked up to see that he was but a few dozen yards from the top. He cursed and swore and summoned up a final surge of desperate desire to infuse groaning muscles with new strength.

Pulling himself upward again, groping with his fingers for the last few crevices in the rock, he saw the top come into view and then he was pulling his long frame over the edge, dragging himself facedown across the flat stone of the passageway. He lay gasping, drawing in deep draughts of air, and felt every muscle in his body trembling, the aftermath of strain beyond their limits. He heard the scraping noise and lifted his head to see the Ovaro looking on with patient watchfulness. He smiled with a rush of gratefulness and pushed to his feet and slowly pulled himself into the saddle. He saw where the *banditos* had turned and gone back down from the rock hills and he kept the Ovaro at a walk as he followed. Only when he reached the gentle ground at the bottom did he put the horse into a trot as he followed the hoofprints.

They stayed together and had headed south and as he followed he soon realized they had tailed Dulcy's prints. The thoughts leapfrogged instantly through his mind. They had lied to her about keeping him a prisoner. It appeared as though they were going to give Dulcy another surprise. This time her clever, careful plans were going to backfire. He put the horse into a gallop as he crossed low, rolling terrain, suddenly heavy with black oak. The trail cut through an opening in the clusters of oak and he had just crossed over a low rise when he heard the shots, two in quick succession, then two more, spaced apart. He sent the Ovaro into a knot of oaks, dismounted and went forward on foot, crouching as he ran to a hogback that let him peer into a small hollow with two big oaks facing each other across a small, clear space.

One of the *banditos* lay lifeless on the ground and he saw Aquena and two of his men crouched behind tree trunks, their backs to him, their attention on the oak across from them. "We will let you go alive, *muchacha,* even though you killed Domas. We just want to have a good time with you. Don't you like a good time?" Aquena called.

"Come get me, you bastards," Dulcy's voice called from the oak.

"You will be sorry if we must do that," Aquena said, a touch of chiding in his tone.

"I'm sorry now," Dulcy flung back and Fargo's glance swept the *banditos* again. One lay dead but there was one missing and his eyes immediately moved to the edges of the oak that sheltered Dulcy. He had to wait almost a minute before he spotted the figure crawling forward at the rear of the tree. The man had worked his way around to come up behind her and Fargo saw him disappear inside the tree branches. Dulcy's voice came a few moments later, a half-scream and then a curse.

"I've got the bitch," the man's voice called out and Fargo drew the blade from its calf-holster. He needed to get his hands on a sixgun and there was but one way to do it. Aquena and the other two men rose and started across the clear patch of ground, their attention on the man who stepped from the oak holding Dulcy. Fargo darted forward on silent steps and his arm rose as, using all the power in his shoulder, he flung the double-edged blade. He was still darting forward, watching it streak through the air as it slammed into one of the two men following Aquena. It sunk through his back to the hilt, penetrating right between his shoulder blades. He stiffened for a moment before he flung his arms out, uttered a gargling cry as he fell forward. Aquena and the other man half turned to glance back but Fargo was already at the figure on the ground, yanking the revolver from his holster.

He fired from his knees as Aquena's surprised curse exploded and was cut off by the bullet that slammed into his midsection. The other man tried to dive away as he pulled his gun out. His body shook in midair as Fargo's bullet crashed through his side and he fell facedown on the ground to lay still. Fargo rose to one knee to face the man holding Dulcy in front of him, a gun shoved into her side. "I'll kill her," the *bandito* shouted.

"And I'll kill you," Fargo said almost offhandedly.

The man paused for a moment. "You want her alive? Drop the gun," he said but Fargo heard the fear in his voice.

"Doesn't matter a hell of a lot to me," Fargo said. "But the only way you're going to stay alive is to let her go."

Dulcy had the sense not to struggle, he saw, as the man wrestled with his choices. Fargo kept the revolver aimed but he cursed silently. There was enough room for a single, absolutely accurate shot, a marksman's shot. He could do it if he had his Colt but that was still in Aquena's belt and he didn't know the gun he held well enough to risk it. He had to lean on the one thing he had going for him, the man's fear. "You've got ten seconds to stay alive, *amigo*," he said calmly.

"You'll shoot," the man said.

"Not if you let her go," Fargo said.

"Drop your gun first," the man said, bargaining out of fear, his voice with a quiver in it.

"Five seconds," Fargo said.

"*Roñoso*," the man shouted, drew the gun from Dulcy's side and began firing at Fargo. Dulcy dropped to the ground as Fargo rolled way from the bullets that slammed into the ground. He came up on his stomach firing, emptied the gun, and saw the man turn first one way and then the other as the bullets slammed into him until the strange little dance ended and he crumpled to the ground. Fargo rose, tossed the empty gun aside, and grimaced. "You never know what a scared man will do," he bit out as he paused at the lifeless form of Aquena and pulled the Colt from his belt.

Dulcy had pushed herself to her feet and let a whistling sigh escape her. "That was close," she said. "I owe you."

"We'll start with the questions you're going to answer," he said. "And don't try to con me. I'm not too happy with you now."

"Go ahead," Dulcy Abbot said.

"Not here," he said. "Let's get your horse," He walked with her to the other side of the oak and picked up the rifle on the ground along the way. He emptied the shells from it and handed it to her and stuffed it into a rifle holster when they reached the horse. He whistled and the Ovaro came at a trot, "Ride," he growled as he swung into the saddle.

6

He found a small pond surrounded by cedar elms and half sat on a rock as Dulcy Abbot regarded him with a stare of reproach. "What are you so angry about? I'm the one who ought to be angry. You've been chasing me," she said.

"You just left me to be killed, honey," he told her.

"That's not so," she protested hotly. "I paid them to keep you prisoner for a month."

"So you did," Fargo grunted.

"What more do you want?" she snapped.

He turned an icy smile on her. "You killed one of them when they caught up to you," he said. "How'd you manage that?"

"I kept watching my tail and when I saw them I knew something had gone wrong and I was ready for them," Dulcy said.

"Why'd you keep watching your tail?" he asked mildly.

"I always watch my tail," she said.

"Try again," Fargo said and he saw the flash of realization touch her face before her eyes narrowed at him. "Or maybe you'd like me to answer that," he said. "You were watching your tail because you had a gut feeling they wouldn't keep the bargain." She didn't answer but he saw the moment of uncomfortableness slide through her face. "What does that say, honey?" he asked, his voice hardening.

Her eyes flashed defiance. "It says I tried to do the right thing by you."

"It says you knew the chances that it might go wrong and it didn't stop you from hanging me out to dry," Fargo threw back.

She looked away. "We do what we have to do," she said.

"That's right. And what I have to do is bring you back," he said.

"You can hear my side, first," she said and sat against a log stump and stretched and her slender waist moved with catlike grace. The late-day sun bathed her handsome face as she lifted her head and he saw the taut beauty of her again. "You afraid to?" she challenged. "You afraid you might believe me?"

"Not afraid of that," he said. "I can tell real from fake, truth from lies."

"I'm sure of that. A man who didn't fall for all the things I set up won't likely to be fooled," she said and he shot her a hard glance. Flattery was a disarming weapon. She'd not be above using it, he was certain. But her face showed only calmness. Yet he wouldn't put it past her. In fact, there was little he'd put past Dulcy Abbot. But one fact stuck inside him. Any young woman who had done all she had done had to have a damned powerful reason for it. And Rob Abbot had concocted a giant hoax to get him here, he reminded himself. Maybe he'd lied about more.

"I'm listening," he said and she rose and paced back and forth for a moment.

"Nothing's like what he told you," she said.

"How do you know what your pa told me?" he asked.

She halted, faced him, and uttered a wry snort. "We can start right there. He's not my pa. Rob Abbot's my stepfather," she said and Fargo felt the moment of surprise lift his brows.

"Why'd you take two thousand dollars, stepfather or not?" Fargo questioned.

"The money I took was mine," she said.

"I'll set that aside, seeing as it's your word against his and nothing more," Fargo told her. "Why are you trying to wreck the business?"

"Is that what he told you?" Dulcy frowned and he nodded. "Another lie. My mother's will made me a partner in the business with him until I was twenty-one," she said.

"That's what he said."

"Did he also tell you she made a codicil to her will that said I got everything when I turned twenty-one?" Dulcy shot back.

"No," Fargo admitted.

"Well, she did, only he destroyed it so he didn't have to turn everything over to me when I reached twenty-one," Dulcy said.

"So you decided to run and bring the business down on his head, knowing he couldn't run it without your signature on things," Fargo finished.

"No, that's not why I ran," she said.

"It was the gambling man," Fargo offered.

A furrow creased the smoothness of her forehead. "What gambling man?"

"The one you've been chasing. He told me you were hooked on him," Fargo said.

"God, he really painted a whole picture, didn't he. There's no gambling man. There is a man I'm chasing down. He used to work for my mother. He's the only living person who knows she made a copy of that codicil and where she hid it. That's why I've got to find him," Dulcy said.

Fargo let a long sigh escape his lips as he studied Dulcy Abbot. "It's all still your word and his. He says you were made a partner. You say you got everything at twenty-one. He says you stole from him. You say you didn't. He says you went off chasing a gambling man. You say there's no gambling man. All words."

"No, not just words. Think about the gambling man story. What gambling man would be out here in this stinking, hell-hole country with nothing but crummy little towns? If I were chasing a gambling man I'd be in Dallas or St. Louis or New Orleans," she said and Fargo let his lips purse in thought. Her point was a good one, he conceded silently, a damn good one. But she was smart, he reminded himself, smart enough to make good points.

"What's his name, this feller you're chasing," he asked and peered hard at her to catch the slightest moment of uncertainty or hesitation. But there was none.

"Harry Kelso. Anything else?" she said instantly, her eyes challenging.

"Yes," Fargo told her. "It took a lot of time, money, and wheedling to set up all the things you did. Why didn't you just spend that time running?"

"Because I knew it'd take a lot of looking and a lot of time to find Harry Kelso. I couldn't do it knowing he was sending people after me," she said. "I thought I'd done more than enough to turn away anyone he sent. You sure surprised the hell out of me."

"You still had a good start. Why'd you hole up for three weeks in Longley?" he pressed.

"I needed help, riders to scout more territory than I could alone and a base for them to report. That's when I hired those *banditos* to fan out and bring me back whatever they picked up."

"What happened with the mayor and the sheriff?" he questioned with new sharpness.

She gave a grim snort. "When I got the message from Anita that you had reached that far, I couldn't be sure she could pull off getting you to take her back. The messenger reported you were a big man riding a big Ovaro. That's when I went to the mayor and the sheriff. I'd already buttered them up with some cash favors."

"Your usual technique," Fargo interrupted.

"That's right," she admitted. "If you reached Longley I wanted them to arrest you, find some charge, and hold you for at least a month. I gave them the description of you and the Ovaro. They agreed if I'd go to bed with them. Imagine that, the bastards? I told them to go to hell but they decided they'd have me right there and then. They grabbed me and started to take me. When I got a chance to, I grabbed the sheriff's gun. The idiot was still wearing it and I shot them both."

"Then high-tailed it from town," Fargo said.

"Of course. I don't expect ever to be in Longley again and I'm betting the sheriff will keep it pretty much in town. I'll bet he's got plenty of dirt on the stick himself," Dulcy said. She drew a deep breath and watched as Fargo regarded her with a long frown. "That's all of it," she said. "Now what?"

He found himself unable to make up his mind about her. "I don't know," he admitted. "You've explained away some things, made others make sense, and made some points of your own. But you're still asking me to take your word for everything and I can't just do that. It's asking too much."

"I'll do better than that," Dulcy said. "I'll hire you to help me find Harry Kelso. I'll pay you more than Rob has. We find Harry Kelso and you'll know everything I've told you is the truth."

"I made a deal with Rob Abbot, even though he tricked me into it. I don't go back on my word," Fargo said.

"I'm not asking you to do that. Just help me find Harry Kelso, first. Then you'll know who's lied to you, Rob Abbot or me," she said.

Fargo turned her proposal in his mind. Rob Abbot had set him up, lied to him. Maybe he had lied about a lot more. But Fargo knew he couldn't simply swallow Dulcy's answers, either. But she had given him more than enough to wonder about. Maybe she did deserve a little more time. He fastened a penetrating stare at her. "I'm going to cut you some rope," he said. "We don't find Harry Kelso, I'm taking you back. We do find him, I'm taking you back, whether he backs up your story or whether he doesn't. It makes no difference. I'm taking you back, with him if you want. I'll do my job. You can settle the rest yourselves."

"That's fair enough," Dulcy said.

"You've any leads on Kelso?" Fargo questioned.

"When he worked for my mother he used to talk about a cabin he had near Frio Canyon and he always wanted to go back there sometime. I think that's where he went. Those *banditos* heard that someone who might have been him was seen near Longhorn Cavern. That'd be on the way to Frio Canyon," she said.

"That's where we go, then," he said as dusk settled down. "We stay the night here and start at dawn," he said and she nodded, stepped forward, and put a hand on his arm.

"Thanks," she said.

"Don't need thanks. I'm doing it to satisfy myself," he said gruffly.

"Nothing wrong in that," she said with a warm smile. The smile vanished when he strode to her dark bay and began to rummage through her saddlebag. "What are you doing?" she asked sharply.

"Taking this," he said, pulling out a revolver, a Remington-Beals six-shot single-action piece, he saw.

"How'd you know I had that?" Dulcy frowned, coming up to him.

"No one who plans and prepares the way you do would make this trip without a sixgun," he said. "Now, I'll take the rest of the shells for that rifle." She tossed him a small glower as she reached into a leather sack and brought out a box of shells. "Thanks," he smiled and walked to the Ovaro and put the gun and shells into his own saddlebag.

"You're a strange one, Fargo. You're willing to help me prove I'm not lying to you, yet you don't trust me," she said and looked hurt.

"Memory problem," he said and she frowned back. "I keep remembering how you hung me out to dry when push came to shove," he said.

"It's different now," Dulcy said.

"We do what we have to do. Your words, honey. You might decide there's something else you have to do," he smiled almost affably.

She continued to look hurt. "You can trust me. I'll make you see that," she said.

"You work on it," he said as he unsaddled the Ovaro. "Got anything to eat? I've some jerky you can have."

"I've dried beef strips in my pouch," she said and when he set out his bedroll under a half-moon she came to sit beside him. The night stayed warm and when she finished eating she rose and looked down at him. "I'm going to take a dip in the pond," she said.

"Now?" he asked.

"You can see too much in the morning," she said and he watched her take a towel and a robe from her pack and walk the dozen yards to the pond. He watched her shed her clothes, and wondered if she realized how well the moonlight let him see. She turned her back to him as she pulled off the last garment, a half-slip, and he glimpsed a long, lean body and a flat rear as she disappeared into the pond. He listened to her splashing in the water as he undressed down to his underdrawers and stretched out on the bedroll. She held the large towel around her after she came out and went into the trees, where he heard the soft sound of cloth rubbing against skin.

She had the robe on when she came with a blanket and spread it beside his bedroll. He looked across at her and saw she was on one elbow, her eyes taking in the smooth muscled beauty of his body. The top of the dark blue robe hung loose and he caught the long line of the edge of one breast and in the moonlight her handsome face was softened to give her a more vulnerable kind of loveliness. "I'm glad for one thing," she said, a hint of laughter in her voice.

"What's that?" he asked.

"You trust me enough not to tie me up so's I won't run away," she said.

"Trust's got nothing to do with it," he said.

"No?" she said, putting disappointment into the single word.

"You're much too smart to try and run away. You know I'd catch up to you," he said.

She laughed, a low, pleasant sound. "So true. Good night, Fargo," she said.

" 'Night," he returned and listened to her settle down. She was asleep when he looked across at her, on her side, facing him, a long, lovely calf uncovered and he realized that Dulcy Abbot was even more of an enigma than she had been.

7

When morning came he rose, washed in the pond, and was half dressed when Dulcy woke. She sat up, pulled together the robe that had loosened to show a soft-lined thigh. She rose to her feet and managed to look cool and regal as she disappeared into the trees. When she returned she was dressed, changed into a tan shirt, her long brown hair hanging loose and full. They breakfasted on papaw and headed south. She rode well, one with her horse, moving easily, her breasts hardly swaying under the tan shirt.

"Every minute counts, Fargo," she said. "Harry Kelso was an old man when he left after Mother died. He was failing, then. I only hope he's still alive."

"What if he isn't?" Fargo questioned. "You look some more for the copy of that codicil?"

"If I can. If Abbot doesn't get rid of me. He can't afford to let me find it. That's why he wants you to bring me back," she said and paused. "I know you think I'm exaggerating," she added.

"I'm not thinking anything yet," Fargo said.

She gave him a sidelong glance. "That's fair. I was angry that he hired the one person able to find me, but now maybe I'm glad it's you," she said and sounded more like a pleased little girl than the very clever and determined young woman he'd been pursuing. He led the way across terrain that alternated between flat stretches and low, rock-filled hills. But a frown began to cross his brow as he halted to examine the lines of hoofprints that moved back and forth across the flatland, some clustered together, others in single file. "Indian prints?" she asked.

"Too damn many of them," he nodded. "All the prints pretty fresh. I don't like it."

"Let's ride faster and get away from here."

"Not faster. Slower," he said.

"Slower?" she frowned.

"Riding faster means not seeing and not seeing means getting killed. We ride slow and careful and keep our eyes open," Fargo said and moved the pinto forward at a walk as he swept the terrain ahead and on both sides with narrowed eyes. A line of hackberry appeared and he moved inside the trees until they came to an end and he motioned Dulcy to a halt. She followed his gaze to where a knot of horsemen were tiny forms in the distance. Fargo stayed at the edge of the trees until the riders disappeared and then cautiously nosed out into the open. The land stayed flat and open for perhaps a half-mile, he estimated, and, waving at Dulcy, he put the pinto into a gallop to where the rock formations rose.

He was perspiring when they reached the hill and climbed up into the tall rocks and he knew it was not from the ride and the sun alone. He halted at a spot that let him see into the distance where the land again became flat and almost treeless. A mile of it this time, he guessed, and he squinted into the sky for a moment. The day had another few hours to it and he scanned the flatland again. Nothing moved and he was fairly certain there was another low hill of rocks at the far side. "We'll make another run for it," he said unhappily. He led the way from the rocks and again set off at a gallop. Dulcy stayed close behind him and he was grateful to see the hill with the rock formations rise as he neared the end of the flatland. He rode into the rocks and halted as Dulcy came alongside him and dusk began to gather.

"We made it," she breathed.

"Yes, but we won't keep being lucky. From now on we ride by night and sleep by day," he said.

"We won't make much time riding by night," Dulcy said.

"No, but we might make Longhorn Caverns with our scalps," he said and dismounted. Dulcy slid from her horse to sit against a rock across from him, grim annoyance in her face. "Is finding that codicil worth getting killed?" he asked.

"I never planned on getting killed," Dulcy said.

"You're sure flirting with it in this territory," he told her.

"Are you saying you don't want to go on?" she asked.

"I'm saying that's what I ought to do, not what I'm going to do," he muttered.

"Thank you," she said softly and reached out, her hand pressing his arm for a moment as the night began to descend.

"Let's ride," he said and rose to climb into the saddle. Dulcy followed him from the rocks and he moved southward across the flat open land as the moon surfaced. He was following no prints so the dark made no difference. All he had to do was ride south and he used the moon as a guide. He set as hard a pace as he dared in the night shadows and the moon was more than halfway across the sky when Dulcy called out.

"Can't we rest awhile?" she asked.

"No. Exhaustion will help you sleep through the day," he said, more gruffly than he had intended. She said nothing more and rode in silence beside him and when the moon dipped below the horizon he swung west to where a rock-filled hill rose. Slowing, he moved up a narrow passage through the rocks to halt in a small circle surrounded by tall granite and sandstone formations that afforded a perfect, hidden-away spot. He heard Dulcy groan in tiredness as she swung from the horse. The sun came up quickly, instantly hot, and he clambered up one of the rocks to peer down at the terrain below. They weren't very high up but the spot was well hidden and he was satisfied.

He slid down to the stone circle and set down his bedroll. Dulcy, a blanket in her hand, peered up at the surroundings. "There's no shade here at all," she frowned.

"You're tired enough to sleep without shade," he said.

"I'll roast to death sleeping in clothes in this sun," she protested.

"That's right," he said.

"Meaning what exactly?" she frowned.

"Who said anything about sleeping in clothes," he said as he began to unbutton his shirt. She blinked as she watched him take the shirt off and toss it down, undo his gunbelt and place it at the edge of his bedroll. He started to undo his jeans when she interrupted.

"Is this your answer?" she frowned.

"You have a better one?" he said as he shed the jeans and stretched out on the bedroll in his underdrawers, his muscled torso glistening in the sun. She stared at him for a moment before she strode through a passage in the rocks and he flexed the tired muscles of his body. When she returned she was in pink bloomers and she had tied the shirt into a flat strip that covered most of her breasts. But not enough, he saw through half-closed eyes, to the long, lovely swell of their fullness. Her bare midriff was flat and nicely modeled and the bloomers clung to reveal long, well-shaped thighs and a flat, tight rear. She had a body that echoed the handsome tautness of her face, he decided, and saw that she stood over him, glaring down at him.

"I'm wondering if you planned it this way," she said.

He kept his eyes half closed. "Don't flatter yourself, honey. All I planned was a way to stay alive. Now I'm getting some sleep," he said. She turned away and he watched her lie down on the blanket, on her side again. The band of fabric she'd fastened around her breasts slipped enough for him to glimpse more of their creamy white softness. But his body demanded sleep and he closed his eyes and shut the world out almost instantly.

The sun burned down, hot, yet soothing, and there was enough of a faint wind to make the circle of rocks not impossibly uncomfortable. He had no idea how long he had slept when his wild-creature hearing woke him, the faint sounds drifting to his ears. He pulled his eyes open, squinted into the sky, and saw the sun in the distance. Three quarters of the day had gone and the sound came again, distinct this time and recognizable. His lips drew back in a grimace as he rose to his feet, drawing the Colt from its holster. He crept to the rock nearest him that let him see down to the ground just below. The six horsemen moved almost directly underneath, their long, grease-covered black hair hanging straight, one in the lead wearing a beaded headband. All were bare-waisted but wore makeshift trousers, some cut-down jeans, two in torn U.S. cavalry trousers. Mescalero Apache, he grunted silently. They carried rifles, none new, mostly old army-issue carbines. They halted, their eyes searching the distance. None even glanced upward at the rocks and Fargo allowed a silent grunt of satisfaction as he continued to watch them.

They were just beginning to move on when Dulcy's voice cut through the air. "Oh God, oh yes ... yes. No ... oh, no ... oh God." Fargo whirled to stare back at her. She lay on her back, her eyes closed, fine-lined lips parted and her head moved from side to side as she moaned again. "Oh, oh my God ... oh, yes." He leaped from the rock, landed next to her and clapped a hand over her mouth even as he knew it was too late. She snapped awake, eyes wide as they stared up at him.

"Shit," he swore as he heard the murmur of voices rise from below and he drew his hand from her mouth. She sat up but he was whirling away, leaping to the rock to peer over the top. The Mescalero were staring up at the rocks, the one with the beaded headband gesturing to the passage entrance. They turned their ponies and started for the passage upward and Fargo leaped down from the rock and yanked the big Sharps from the saddle holster as he hissed orders at Dulcy. "Get on your horse," he said and she obeyed, fear in her eyes now. He took the rifle, ran to the top of the passage and dropped to one knee as he waited, listening to the sounds of the Indian ponies as they came upward. The first Mescalero came into sight and he fired, a fraction too quickly and saw the bullet send a hail of stone chips into the air as it hit the edge of a piece of boulder. The Indian withdrew at once and

Fargo heard the murmur of voices, then the sound of their horses backing out of the passage.

He rose and peered over the edge of the rock again. They had halted below and the one with the headband gestured to the other side of the rock formation. He was sending two of his braves to make their way up one of the other passages and Fargo cursed. "They'll trap us in here and I have to reduce the odds," he said to Dulcy. "You ride out of here, ride hard as you can. Be at a gallop when you come out of that passageway," he said.

"They're still bound to catch me," she said.

"Yes, but it'll take them a minute or two. So far as they know you're the only one up here," he said.

"And after they catch me?"

"Don't fight. I'll do the rest," he said. She shot an apprehensive glance at him. "Move, goddammit," he hissed and brought his hand down on the bay's rump. The horse shot forward and Dulcy was on her way down the passage. He climbed into the rock again and had the rifle to his shoulder as Dulcy raced out of the passage and across the flatland below. The four Apache went after her instantly and Fargo followed through the gunsight, aimed at the one bringing up the rear and fired. The Indian's lithe form twisted as it flew from the back of the horse. He had another in his sights already and fired. This time the Mescalero's thick, greased hair flew outward in all directions as the bullet caught him in the side of the head.

The third Apache whirled his pony as he gazed toward the rocks and brought his carbine up to fire. He got off one wild shot and tried to twist his pony away before he fired again, but Fargo's answering shot caught him in the ribs and he bent over in pain before he fell from his mount. But the one with the headband had closed in on Dulcy, his pony alongside the bay as he grabbed at her, one hand extended, clutching a fistful of her hair. She screamed in pain as he yanked her back and flung her to the ground. Fargo was pausing to get a clear shot, his hand on the trigger, when he heard the explosion echo from the rocks. He felt the stinging pain in his cheek as the bullet grazed his head to slam into the rock.

He let himself fall, dropping the rifle, and glimpsed the two Mescalero coming down from the other side of the rock hollow on foot. He fell limply as the rifle clattered its way and he hit the bottom on his side as he drew the Colt. Out of the corner of his eye he saw the two Indians leap down into the open, confident their shot had hit its mark. Fargo waited, muscles tensed, and counted off seconds. He let the two figures come another dozen feet closer before he whirled and brought the Colt up firing, all in one, instant motion. The two Mescalero quivered where they stood, as if struck by lightning, and then collapsed onto each other.

Fargo pulled himself to his feet just as he heard Dulcy's half-scream of pain. He leaped onto the rock to look down and caught a glimpse of the Mescalero disappearing into a crevice in the rocks, on foot and yanking Dulcy with him. Fargo turned back into the rock-bound hill, took a moment to reload, and moved forward toward the creviced passages on the other side of the stone hollow. He traced the Mescalero's movements by Dulcy's gasps of pain. The Indian was making his way up a crevice amid the rocks, trying to go higher, and Fargo moved across a slanted boulder. He leaped to another and he was on the same level as the Indian reached the top of the crevice. Fargo raised the Colt, leveled it at the exit of the crevice, and saw Dulcy appear in his sights.

"It's me, God, don't shoot," she gasped and he caught the shadow of the Indian's arm at her back.

He lowered the Colt and Dulcy was yanked back from the mouth of the crevice and vanished from sight. Fargo raised the Colt again, waited as he wondered what the Mescalero had intended by pushing Dulcy forward. He hadn't used her as a shield from which to fire. Was it just to show him that he had her? Did he hope to provoke him, taunt him into going after her? The questions circled through his mind as he waited and suddenly Dulcy was pushed forward again, helpless fear in her face. The Mescalero stayed down and out of sight but plainly held Dulcy by the wrists. Fargo stayed motionless, easing his finger from the trigger and once again Dulcy was pulled back out of sight into the crevice.

Fargo's finger returned to the trigger and he had to wonder if the Indian was trying to goad him into going after Dulcy. But Fargo didn't move. He kept the Colt aimed at the opening of the crevice. Almost a minute passed and the frown dug deeper into Fargo's brow when Dulcy was pushed into view once more. She was held there, a few moments longer and then pulled back. Fargo cursed silently. Three times the Indian had pushed her into view and three times he had pulled her back. What was he trying to do? Or was he saying something? Did he figure to come charging out firing next time with Dulcy before him, hoping he had lulled his enemy into caution enough to be taken by surprise. Fargo swore again, unable to fathom the Indian's tactics. But the Mescalero were known for their wiliness and Fargo kept his attention riveted on the mouth of the crevice. This time the seconds lengthened and became over a minute. Two minutes passed as Fargo's gaze stayed on the crevice, his lips pulled back, his every muscle tensed. It was his mountain lion hearing that caught the sound, ever so faint.

It was the Mescalero's one mistake. He had hurried a fraction too fast and the barrel of the carbine scraped against the rock for an instant. But Fargo knew he had no time to try and turn. He had only time to fling himself in a sideways dive and he did so as the two shots exploded, slamming into the spot where he had been. He was half rolling and half falling and he came down hard on his right arm and felt the Colt fall from his grip as two more shots followed him. He came to a halt on his back and saw the Mescalero leaping down from the top of the boulder. The Indian had the stock of the carbine raised to smash it down on him and Fargo twisted his body as he kicked out with one leg.

He felt the kick catch the Indian's hurtling form and then the heavy rifle stock graze his ear as it smashed into the stone. Fargo flung himself sideways, but back the other way, into the Indian's legs and the man fell off balance for a moment. But the moment was enough for Fargo to swing himself onto one knee and lash out with a long left hook at the same time. The blow grazed the Apache's jaw yet it had enough force in it to drive him a few steps backward. Fargo took the precious split-second to hurtle himself forward in a flying tackle that brought the Indian down under him. He tried to bring his forearm down into the Apache's throat but, though small, the Indian was quick and wiry and twisted his shoulders enough to half squirt out of Fargo's grip. He got a hand free and Fargo glimpsed the knife in it, rolled away, and just avoided the downward swipe of the blade. He rolled, came up on his feet, and saw the Mescalero coming at him, the hunting knife in one hand, his thick, black hair swinging from side to side as he feinted left and then right and then left again.

Fargo knew he wouldn't have time to get the knife out of its calf-holster and he matched the Indian's feints as he circled. The Mescalero, relying on his quickness, feinted again and then slashed furiously with the blade, upward and then across and Fargo had to duck, twist, and backtrack fast. The man came in slashing again and Fargo gave ground, circling as the Indian continued to slash, each time coming closer to his target. Fargo knew he'd be unable to keep avoiding the slashing blows and as he backed again, his narrowed eyes watching the Indian's every quick movement, he saw that the man ended each slashing series of blows with his body turned slightly to the right.

Fargo circled and tensed his powerful leg and thigh muscles. He knew he'd have but one chance. He was in a half crouch when the Apache came at him again, making three furious slashes of the knife. Fargo dived in low, to the rear and left of his attacker. He brought one boot down hard on the man's bare foot and at the same time he drove both hands into the Indian's back. The Apache uttered a cry of pain as, his ankle twisting and his foot crushed, he fell forward. Fargo reached over his doubled-up body, seized the man's knife arm, and brought it back as he took his boot from the Indian's foot. Using centrifugal force, he swung the Indian in a circle and sent him flying face forward against a straight wall of stone. The Mescalero had just hit against the wall when Fargo, hurling himself forward with all his strength, drove his shoulder into the man's back. He felt the crack of the man's spine and then another sound, a gasping groan, and the Mescalero slid downward against the wall. He crumpled to the ground and Fargo pulled him back by one arm to see the knife blade protruding from his stomach where he'd been driven into it as he was trying to turn it around.

Fargo stepped back and drew a deep breath. It was all painfully clear now. The Mescalero's tactics of showing him Dulcy had been to rivet his attention on the mouth of the crevice while he had climbed up and worked his way to the rear. It had worked, Fargo spit out and ran to the crevice, fearful of what he might find. Dulcy's body lay on the ground a dozen feet from the mouth of the crevice and Fargo dropped to one knee beside her. She was breathing, he saw at once, and he found no rivulet of blood anyway. He turned her head carefully. There was no bruise on her jaw and he nodded with grim admiration. The Indian hadn't killed her, but not out of goodness. With true Mescalero stealth, he knew that if he stabbed her she might well groan and the sound could carry. The sharp impact of a blow might well have carried also. He had cut off her wind until she blacked out and then lowered her silently to the ground.

Fargo gently slapped her face and her eyes slowly opened, stark with fear at first, and then she was clinging to him, drawing in deep, half-sobbed breaths. His hands held the smooth softness of her back and he felt her breasts pressed into his chest. The shirt she had fashioned into a brassiere top somehow still managed to stay up and he finally drew back from her.

"Why the hell didn't you tell me you talked in your sleep?" he asked, anger returning now.

"You never asked me," she shrugged as he pulled her to her feet.

"Well, you damn near got us killed," he growled. "Let's get away from here." He strode off, Dulcy behind him, and led the pinto from the hill to where the bay waited below.

"We still going to ride only by night?" Dulcy asked.

"We ride now and into the night when it comes. Some of their friends will find them. I want to be as far from here as I can when that happens," he said and put the Ovaro into a trot. She hung back a few yards as he rode on and when she caught up he saw that she had put the shirt on properly but let the shirt-tails hang out. There was little more than an hour of daylight left and he concentrated on riding hard across the flatland which had become dotted with clusters of pecan trees and chinquapin oak. When night fell Dulcy's voice came to him from a few paces behind.

"I'm very tired. Can we stop?" she called.

"Not yet. You said every minute counts, remember?" he tossed back and she made no reply. The moon was nearing the midnight sky when he came to a halt under three pecan trees. Dulcy slid from the big bay and he unsaddled the horse as well as the Ovaro.

"Thanks," she said as she fished out her strips of dried beef and sank to the ground. When they finished eating he shook two handfuls of pecans from the tree for dessert and set out his bedroll. Dulcy stretched her blanket beside it, stepped behind one of the tree trunks and returned in a short, light blue cotton night-dress that showed lovely, long legs almost to midthigh.

"That was quite a dream you were having back in the hills," Fargo remarked. "I've heard said that dreams are really memories in sleep."

"Some say they're more wishes than memories," she said.

"What were yours?" he asked.

"I don't know," she answered. "But I'm sorry."

"For not knowing?"

"For not telling you I sometimes talk in my sleep. I just never gave it a thought," she said and sounded really apologetic.

"It's done," he said and she turned to him, sitting very straight, and he saw the tiny pinpoints her breasts pressed into the top of the nightdress.

"I owe you again," she said. "More than I can ever repay."

"I was saving my own neck, too," he said.

"Because of me," Dulcy murmured.

"Doing what I was hired to do," he said.

"Bring me back," she said.

"Bull's eye," he nodded.

"I almost don't care anymore," she said.

"Almost," he echoed and laughed softly. She turned directly to him and her arms rose to slide around his neck and the fine-lined lips pressed into his mouth, warm and promising, until she drew back.

"You stopping?" he slid at her.

"Yes, till the end of almost," she said and sat back. He half laughed and began to undress and she watched him until he was all but naked atop the bed-roll in the warm night and her eyes moved up and down his powerful torso. "You trying to hurry things?" she asked softly.

"Why not?" he shrugged.

"My self-discipline is high," she said.

"Don't doubt that," he muttered as he stretched on his back. Her arm reached out and he felt her hand curl inside his and heard the steady sound of her sleep-filled breathing in seconds. He went to sleep with her hand tight inside his and wondered again at the admixture that was Dulcy Abbot.

8

When morning came he found a stream for washing and ripe, delicious lemon yellow May apple fruit for breakfasting. He weighed the risks of riding by day again against the need to distance themselves from the slain Mescalero and decided to move on. They were well into the afternoon when he crossed a line of wagon tracks that came in from the north and made a wide circle as they headed southwest. He read the tracks with a frown on his brow.

"A coach," he grunted.

"How do you know? It could be just any old Texas cotton-bed," Dulcy said.

"Narrow wheels, a three-horse team. A coach, probably a mud-wagon," he said.

"What's that?" she asked.

"A poor man's Concord, narrower, flat sides, simple joinery throughout, and a helluva lot harder ride," he said. "We'll follow the tracks. They're heading in the right direction."

"You think they'll take us to a town?"

"More likely an overnight stage station but that's fine. A lot of information passes through stage stations," Fargo said and put the Ovaro into a trot. They rode through most of the day and he saw where the stage had stopped to water the horses at two streams along the way. The tracks were fresher now, not more than a few hours old. "I'd say we're getting close to Longhorn Caverns," he ventured and saw the instant excitement come into her face. They went on for another hour, the sun beginning to slide over the horizon and the terrain growing thicker with hawthorn and hackberry, when he saw the stage station come into view. They rode up and he saw the mud-wagon pulled up alongside a flat-roofed, whitewashed stucco building, long and narrow with a half-dozen horses in a corral behind. The stage was unhitched, its three horses tethered nearby, and a man came outside as Fargo dismounted. Medium height with a lean face, a straight nose, and eyes that had seen too much of the world. Straight, black hair was combed down slick and he wore the usual range man's clothes.

"Billy Gattaway," he said, introducing himself with a quick, appraising glance at Dulcy.

"Skye Fargo and Dulcy Abbot," Fargo said.

"Don't usually get visitors except for stage passengers," Gattaway said. "You going to stay the night?"

"Yes. A good bed would be welcome. We've been riding long and hard," Fargo told him.

"We've three stage passengers but we've eight rooms," the man said as he led the way into the station, where Fargo took in a large room set up with a long wood table for dining. The three passengers from the stage were relaxing with drinks and Gattaway introduced them, all three wearing dusty, cheap suits, all road men scouting prospects for their companies, and all eminently forgettable. But very unforgettable was a young woman who came forward, black eyes flashing with interest as she appraised the tall, handsome newcomer.

"I am Rosa," she said with a faint Mexican accent.

But he didn't need the accent to know she was at least half Mexican. The flashing black eyes and glistening black hair and olive tinge to her skin made that plain. On the short side, she wore a scoop-necked white blouse that revealed deep, very full breasts.

"Rosa's here to see to the comfort of our visitors," Gattaway said. "Anything you need, Rosa will see to it if she can."

"Anything?" Fargo remarked.

"That depends on Rosa," the stationmaster said.

Rosa smiled without taking her eyes from Fargo, hands on her hips. Even standing still, Rosa sent out waves of vivacious sensuality. "How about some bourbon?" Fargo said.

"That is a good start, señor," Rosa said and her eyes went to Dulcy.

"Why not?" Dulcy said and Fargo saw the cool arrogance in her handsome face as she turned away, the gesture a dismissal.

Rosa's eyes flashed to Fargo again, full red lips forming a smile that said more than her words. "Maybe we can talk later," she said.

"I believe I'd enjoy that," he said. Her round, slightly fleshy face was pretty in a kind of raw, peasant way. She could channel that electricity that was hers, he saw, as she completely turned it off with the three stage passengers and he smiled inside himself. Rosa would be fun as well as fervent in bed, he wagered as he sat down at a small table where Dulcy had already taken a chair.

"My, you make friends fast," she commented, an edge to her voice.

"She's a friendly young woman," he said.

"I'll bet," Dulcy sniffed. Rosa brought the two bourbons, her eyes flashing only for Fargo and the deep breasts spilling forward as she bent down to set the drinks on the table.

"We don't have many stop by here as *hermoso* as you, señor," Rosa said.

"Compliment of the house?" he laughed.

Her smile came instantly, enveloping in its warmth. "No, just a, how you say, observing."

"Observation," Dulcy corrected coolly.

"*Sí*, observation," Rosa said as she waltzed away, ample hips swinging under a wide, flowered skirt.

"She's bold," Dulcy said.

"Because you're here?" Fargo said.

"That's right. How does she know you're not my man?"

"She knows. A woman such as Rosa doesn't need words. Her judgments come from inside," Fargo said. Two elderly, stooped men appeared carrying bread baskets and dinner plates and Bill Gattaway stepped forward.

"Supper's served, folks," he announced. "Best beef and beans this side of the Rio Grande." Dulcy rose and took a place beside Fargo. The three stage passengers conversed mostly among themselves, though Fargo noticed they cast quick, appreciative glances at Dulcy. The food was indeed good to the taste and hearty and Rosa served red wine from a large, straw-covered pitcher at the end of the meal. Fargo smiled as, when she poured his glass, her full-fleshed thigh pressed against him and she slid a private smile his way. He wasn't the only one who noticed, he realized as Dulcy hissed words at him.

"Bold. I stay with that," she said.

"An unsubtle charm," he remarked and she grunted.

"We're trying to find someone," Dulcy addressed

the stationmaster. "Man by the name of Harry Kelso. Did he by any chance come by this way, maybe a month ago, maybe six months ago?"

"Hell, I don't remember the names of folks who pass in and out of here," Gattaway said.

"You get so many visitors," Dulcy said sarcastically and Gattaway glowered back.

"I just don't pay attention to folks," he muttered. "What'd he look like?"

"Medium height, somewhat stooped, almost white hair, a nose that was once broken right in the middle," Dulcy said.

Gattaway shrugged and Fargo turned as Rosa stepped forward. "There was a *hombre* like that, about two months ago," she said and turned to Gattaway. "Remember, the one who needed money and sold his guitar to me."

"Guitar?" Dulcy echoed, her voice tightening. "Harry Kelso played the guitar. He had the letter H scratched into the back panel."

"Yes, here it is," Rosa said, striding to a corner and holding up a guitar to show the letter marked into the wood.

"Harry Kelso was here. We're on the right track. He had to have been on his way to Frio Canyon," Dulcy said excitedly.

"It seems so," Fargo agreed.

"We'll go on first thing in the morning, get an early start," Dulcy said, her fingers digging into Fargo's arm.

"This has been a worthwhile visit then for you folks," Gattaway said. "More wine, I'd say."

"Good idea," Fargo said and Rosa was at his side at once. Dulcy put her hand over the top of her glass.

"Not for me. I want to have a clear head in the morning and get an early start," she said.

"I'm all for a little celebrating," Fargo said and Rosa filled his glass. He saw Dulcy slide a cool glance at him as he lifted his glass to Rosa. "For your help, *muchacha*," he said and drew a teasing smile. Rosa helped the two elderly men clear away the dishes as Fargo sipped the wine with slow enjoyment.

"I'll pay you now, Mr. Gattaway," Dulcy said to the stationmaster. "That way we can just be on our way come dawn."

"That's fine. Your room's last one down the hallway. Yours is the one before it, Fargo," Gattaway said.

"I'll get my things," Dulcy said, rising.

"I'll see to the horses," Fargo told her as she walked from the room.

"Guess we'll be turning in, too," one of the three stage riders said and the three men rose to leave. Rosa sauntered back into the room, one hand on her hip as she halted in front of Fargo.

"Perhaps you would like to celebrate a little more," she said, flashing the quick, warm smile. "I have not had anything to celebrate in some time."

"Sounds like it might be a good idea," Fargo said. The girl's raw sensuality reached out, direct and unadorned, and he found himself remembering Dulcy's lips on his the night before. It had been a little like one sip of bourbon, stimulating a man's thirst and then nothing else and now he had the entire bottle waiting. "When?" he murmured.

"I'll be finished cleaning up in a little while. Have another wine. Give me a half-hour," Rosa said. "My room is the middle door on the right side of the hallway." Fargo glanced up to see Dulcy in the doorway, her face expressionless and her traveling bag in one hand.

"Good night, Fargo," she said flatly as she went down the long hallway into the other part of the building. Fargo toyed with the wine, sat back in the chair, and listened to the sounds die out in the kitchen. The search for Harry Kelso wasn't over and when it did end he still had to bring Dulcy back. He was not at all certain she'd remain as tractable as she had promised. Hell, he'd not turn his back on a warm, eager package of sensuality such as Rosa. It was against his principles in the first place and he deserved a little enjoyment.

He finished the wine, finally and rose and went outside to see to the Ovaro and Dulcy's bay. He fed both from a feed bin outside the station and tethered them unsaddled to a long rope. When he went inside the house was silent and he made his way down the long corridor, halting at the middle doorway on the right side. He knocked softly. "It's open," Rosa's voice said and he entered a square room, a large bed in one corner and Rosa inside the bed sitting up. She wore a sheer nightgown which let him see the heavy breasts and the dark-tipped points in the glow of a candle. He stepped to her, sank down at the edge of the bed, and saw her eyes had no flash in them now. "I'm sorry, I change my mind," Rosa said.

Fargo was silent for a moment, his gaze taking in her face and he saw her tongue come out to nervously lick her full lips. "That's a lady's privilege," he said. "Sort of sudden, though, isn't it?"

"I'm sorry," she said with a rush of breath and her black eyes were round and contrite. Her hands moved nervously.

"What happened?" Fargo said, watching her closely. "You afraid of something? Gattaway say something to you?"

"No, he doesn't care what I do," Rosa said but the nervousness stayed in her face.

"What is it, then?" Fargo pressed.

"I do not want my throat cut," the girl said. "That's what she said she'd do, that *mujer* of yours."

"Dulcy?" Fargo frowned in surprise and Rosa nodded vigorously.

"She knock. I thought it was you. She told me if I spend the night enjoying you she would cut my throat," the girl said. "She was cold as ice water. She would do it, that one."

Fargo stared at Rosa. She was definitely afraid. Dulcy had clearly gotten to her and he swore under his breath as he rose to his feet. Rosa's hand shot out and curled around his arm, fear still in her face. "She tell me not to say anything to you. I am sorry but I cannot lay with you . . . I cannot. I am too *temerosa*," she said. He nodded and stepped back.

"Another time maybe. *Yo comprendo*," he said and strode from the room with the anger rising inside him. He reached the last door in the corridor in a dozen long strides, closed his hand around the knob, and turned. The door came open and he stepped into the room, one much like Rosa's with a candle glowing atop a small dresser. The figure atop the bed lay unmoving and he stepped to the bedside, reached down, and yanked her upright by one arm. "You're not asleep, dammit," he bit out.

Dulcy glared up at him, the short nightdress around her. "I'm not now," she snapped. "What are you doing in my room?"

"You know damn well what I'm doing here. You have your goddamn nerve," Fargo rasped.

"I want you fresh and ready to ride hard come

morning, not exhausted from enjoying yourself all night," Dulcy said.

"Who I screw and for how long is none of your damn business," he flung back.

She shrugged, unflustered. "That's not how I see it," she said.

"I don't give a damn how you see it. You've no right stopping me from having a good time if I feel like it. Who the hell do you think you are?" he demanded.

She shrugged again. "Go ahead then, enjoy yourself all you want," she said.

"You know I can't. You scared the hell out of her," he flung back, paused, and caught the pleased little flicker that touched her eyes. "You little bitch," he said, curling one hand around the back of her neck. "Maybe you'd like to make up for what you did."

"Is that what you want?" she asked as he pulled her closer.

"Why not?" he muttered.

"Why not?" she echoed and her arms came around his neck, her mouth pressing his as she lay back on the bed, pulling him with her. He felt the moment of surprise as she wriggled and the nightdress came off and her eyes held a defiance in them. As he pulled off his clothes he took in breasts that were longish but very round and creamy white with a lovely curve to their contours, each topped with a light pink small tip against a circle of matching pink. Her hips moved and the garment fell away completely, revealing a long, lean torso with the rib cage faintly visible and a long, narrow waist that curved into a flat abdomen with a tiny indentation in the center. Narrow hips flowed down to a surprisingly bushy, jet black triangle, deep and fluffy in the center. She held her long, lean legs tightly together, which was strangely provocative.

His mouth came to hers, pressed hard, tongue moving out, exploring, messenger of messengers, and Dulcy made eager little noises as she answered. His head moved down onto the creamy white breasts. "Yes, oh yes, yes ... Jesus, yes," Dulcy breathed as he let his lips draw on one small pink tip, tongue circling the soft nipple as he felt it rise and grow firmer. Dulcy sighed out small gasps of pleasure and urging as he continued to gently pull and suck. His hand moved downward, exploring a soft path across the flat abdomen, and then strayed across her belly and hips, and back again to reach the dense, bushy triangle.

"Oh yes, oh yes ... Jesus, yes," Dulcy cried out and her legs moved from side to side, still held together tightly, and moving in unison. His hand crept into the bushy, jet nap, pressed down on the Venus mound, already swollen and waiting and Dulcy cried out again and her long legs moved almost frantically back and forth together and her hips twisted with the motion. His mouth had found hers again and she opened her lips wide, embracing, drawing him in, entreaties of the portals even as his hand crept downward, deeper under the edge of the dense V, and he felt the wetness of her. "Oh God ... Jeeeesus," Dulcy half screamed and the long legs held together suddenly fell apart, quivered, slapped together again and fell apart again. His hand explored, fingertips touching wet softness, and Dulcy was crying out with words that became only sounds and sounds that became echoes of ecstasy.

Her hips rose, bucked spasmodically and her hands dug into his buttocks. "Please, please, now, oh God, take me, take me," she gasped and as he rolled over her, his warm, firm-soft flesh touching the dark portal, her gasped cries became screams of anticipation. Her legs stiffened, and she brought her hips up as she dug her heels into the bed, the consummate offering, the plea wrapped in desire. He slid forward slowly, into the dark, damp funnel and felt the liquescent warmth flowing around him. Dulcy surged forward with an inner sweet honey embrace, welcome of welcomes, and the long, lean calves rose to clasp around him. "Yeeees, oh God, yeeeees," she moaned and rose upward again with him and now her hands groped, found his neck, and drew his face down to her breasts.

She held him there as he felt her torso begin to quiver. A series of tremors coursed through her, which soon grew stronger and turning into bucking, heaving spasms. The sound was torn from deep inside her as she rubbed her breasts back and forth under his lips. "Now, now, oh God now . . . ," Dulcy groaned and he felt himself being carried along with her, peaking with her, delicious explosions that erased all else as the flesh encompassed the world. Finally, half choking out breaths, she ceased her wild tremors and fell back onto the bed, small quivers still rippling through her until finally they halted, too. Her eyes opened and she stared at him as if slowly regaining consciousness. "Jeez, I might have known," she said.

"Does this mean the end of almost?" he asked blandly.

"No," she smiled. "Good try. This means you made me feel guilty."

"Good," he said and settled down beside her, one hand curled around her right breast. She made contented little noises as his thumb lightly caressed the pink tip and she turned on her side, propped up on one elbow to focus an appraising stare at him.

"What if we don't find Harry Kelso? Would you still take me back, after this?" she questioned.

"Yes," he said. "I never let pleasure interfere with business."

She offered a wry smile. "I guess I might have known that, too," she said and he nodded as he lay back. She came to him, resting her breasts on his chest as her hand moved down his body, fingers inquiring their way past his groin and then coming to his quiet maleness, closing and grasping. She uttered a tiny gasp of delight. Her mouth came to his as her hand caressed, toyed, stroked, explored further, and returned again. Little sounds of enjoyment came from her lips and then, as he responded, rising and filling with surging pulsation, she gave a half-scream of triumph and she was pulling herself across him, atop him, rubbing the very dense, fluffy triangle back and forth over him. Her thighs drew up and she pushed herself to him, demanding, all hungry wanting, and her scream sounded as she slid over him, absorbing, encompassing, sensation devouring sensation, and she moved faster, deeper, sliding back and forth until her entire body shook and her round breasts bounced and swayed.

He lifted himself and surged with her and when her cries spiraled to their climax she fell over him, clinging, breasts falling into his face as her body bucked and leaped and the moment of time standing still came again.

Finally she lay limp over him, small sighing sounds of total satisfaction coming from her lips until finally they halted and there was only the steady breathing of deep sleep. He lay awake for a moment longer, his thoughts on the enigmatic, passionate creature who lay against him. Had she really terrorized Rosa for the reason she had given? Or did she just want to stop him from sleeping with Rosa? He wouldn't put the last past her. He knew something else, also. She'd never admit it. He was smiling as he closed his eyes.

9

They left the stage station before anyone else was up, taking a handful of biscuits on the table, and rode southwest with the new day's sun. It was only when he stopped at a water-filled sinkhole for the horses that he spoke to her. "Tired?" he asked mildly.

"Not at all," she said. "You enjoy yourself?"

"Oh, I did," he smiled. "I'd say we should both be happy."

"I am," she said.

"And you got your way last night," he said.

"Whatever that means," she said evenly.

"Whatever that means," he repeated.

"No need to go to Longhorn Caverns now. I have the first real lead. We'll head straight for Frio Canyon. I don't want to waste another minute, now," Dulcy said and set off in a fast trot. He stayed with her as they rode across low hills, some rocky, most now covered with scraggly hawthorn and Texas pistachio. A plain opened up in front of them, dry and sandy, almost desert, but plentifully dotted with piñon. They made good time crossing the sandy terrain but his gaze never stopped scanning the distant piñons with their rounded crowns and dense branches. But Fargo slowed the horses to a walk as the sun grew scorching, the packed, sandy soil reflecting its rays. "Damn,"

Dulcy muttered. "Maybe we should have gone west farther."

"This is the most direct way," Fargo said and wiped the back of his neck. By the time they had gone another few hours, Dulcy's shirt was wet with perspiration and clinging to her breasts as a wet leaf clings to a stone. The enervating heat kept him from pursuing the thoughts that crossed his mind. They had gone into the afternoon, the sun burning without relief when his near-falcon eyesight found two small, dark objects in the distance. He steered the pinto to draw closer to the objects on the surface of the sand, Dulcy beside him, his gaze squinted through the haze of heat. His brow furrowed and the furrow deepened as he reined the horse to a halt.

"My God," Dulcy breathed as the objects became the swollen, blistered heads of two men, so reddened they seemed almost black, both buried in the sand up to their chins. "Good God, who would do that?" she breathed.

"It's an old Mescalero torture," Fargo said as he peered at the two heads. "They're still alive," he said. "They've been there most of the day, I'd guess." He moved the pinto toward the two men when Dulcy's hand caught at his arm.

"What are you going to do?" she asked.

"Save them, if I can. I told you, they're still alive. Maybe we can keep them that way till we get them someplace. There'll be another stage station at Longhorn Caverns. We can't leave them."

"I can," Dulcy said coldly and he paused to look at her.

"You mean that, don't you?" he said with a mixture of sadness and surprise.

"Yes," she said.

"What the hell are you all about?" he asked. "I was beginning to have more than respect for you. I was beginning to like you."

"Look, they're barely alive. Their brains must be scorched. They won't last till we find a place and we'll have lost days," Dulcy said.

"Harry Kelso's been hiding this long, a few more days won't make any difference to him. It will to these poor devils," Fargo said and sent the Ovaro forward. He reached the two victims, some ten feet apart from each other and heard Dulcy following. He couldn't tell if the men were young or old, their faces were so swollen and blistered.

Canteen in hand, he dropped to the ground beside the nearest man and tilted his head backward and slowly poured water past the blistered lips. The man swallowed and a gasping rattle came from his throat. Fargo went to the next man and did the same. "There's a short-handled spade in my pack. Get it out and start digging them out," he said over his shoulder to Dulcy.

"This is crazy. Can't you see that?" she said.

"I don't go by everything I see. I wouldn't have caught you if I did," he said and heard her hiss as she dismounted. He was pouring another sip of water down the second man's blistered mouth when the shot rang out and the swollen head exploded as though it were an overripe melon. Fargo whirled as he dived and saw the four Mescalero drop from the branches of the piñon pine a dozen yards away. He cursed as he knew there was time only to leap onto the Ovaro and send the horse into a gallop.

He glimpsed Dulcy, frozen in surprise, and the Mescalero running at her, but he knew he'd never get away if he took the precious seconds to reach her. He flattened himself over the pinto's neck and caught sight of two more Mescalero appearing in the distance, leading four riderless ponies. Dulcy's scream of fury followed him, cut short as the Indians reached her. They'd be content with their prize, he knew, and he kept the pinto full out until he reached a low ridge where he halted some half-mile away. He sent a stream of curses flying into the air and pounded on the saddle horn with his fist.

It had been his fault. He had swept the terrain for a glimpse of Indian ponies and saw none. Now he knew why. They had turned an old Mescalero torture into a wily trap. He should have been more careful but he had let Dulcy's icy coldness surprise and unsettle him. No excuses made, just the fact that he had let it happen, and he swore into the burning sun again. He forced himself to stay and wait. He let enough time go by before he nosed the Ovaro from the ridge and began to retrace his steps. They wouldn't kill her, not for a while, at least. She was too special a prize. They might eventually take her to their main camp. He let himself ride slowly, eyes scanning the dry, sandy terrain. He finally reached the place where their two victims were now only grotesque objects in the sand.

The second man had succumbed to the burning sun and Fargo studied the hoofmarks nearby. They had gone off with Dulcy's bay in the center of their ponies. They'd turned east and he stayed far behind as he followed. When the searing sun began to slide beyond the horizon, the sandy flatland turned to a series of low hillocks dotted with hackberry and with the ground well covered by mesquite bushes. The sun went down and the terrible scorching stopped but the night stayed hot and dry and as darkness fell he dismounted and began to trail the hoofprints by foot. It was slow-going but he was on their trail when the new moon rose to supply only a fraction more light. The prints moved over a hillock and when he reached the top he came to a halt, the sound of their voices drifting up to him. He moved forward at a crouch to peer down the other side of the hillock.

The Mescalero had decided to camp for the night in the narrow dip at the bottom of the slope and he spied a small stream running through the area. He sought out Dulcy at once. They had tied her to a stake by the wrists with her ankles bound together, long, round breasts bare and her half-slip torn so most of her body was exposed. Her clothes were strewn on the ground near her. Her captors were a dozen yards or so from her, exchanging guttural bursts of talk as they prepared to sleep.

For the most part they simply stretched out on the warm ground, their weapons beside them, and Fargo's gaze went to their ponies. They were tethered together on a long, rawhide strip that was in turn wrapped around a low branch of a hackberry. Dulcy's bay was tied with the other horses, all about fifteen yards from the stake were Dulcy was bound. Fargo sank to one knee and waited as, one by one, the Mescalero fell asleep. When the sounds of their heavy breathing reached him, interspersed with an occasional snore, he carefully led the Ovaro around the edge of the camp-site close to where the ponies were tethered. Using his lariat, and working slowly and carefully, he began to hobble each of the Apache ponies, pausing when they whinnied to stay frozen in the dark shadows. He was almost finished when one of the Mescaleros came awake, raising his head and peering into the darkness and then falling back to sleep again.

Fargo finished the last horse, quickly examined his work, and saw that the six ponies were well hobbled, left foreleg ankle tied to right hindleg ankle, giving each horse enough room to move but not enough to run. He hung the rest of the lariat around his neck and half crawled his way to where Dulcy lay on her side. She was only dozing and woke as he neared her, frowned for a moment, and then recognized him and he put a finger to her lips. With the knife from his calf-holster, he cut the rawhide thongs binding her and she reached for her clothes to start putting them on. His hand closed around her arm and stopped her and he shook his head at her. She wanted to argue with him but the hardness in his eyes stopped her and she followed him, moving on hands and knees as he made his way back to the line of ponies.

He took a last glance at his work and estimated it would take the Apache at least three minutes to discover their ponies had been hobbled and to untie the rope hobbles. He had tied the ropes low enough on the fetlock so the ropes could just be cut without the danger of the horse stepping on the dangling ends as he ran. Dulcy, beside the bay, started to pull on clothes and again he stopped her and motioned her into the saddle. She climbed onto the horse, stuffed her clothes into the saddlebag, and glared at him as he silently stepped to where the Ovaro waited. He swung onto the saddle and slowly walked the horse away from the campsite into a line of hackberry. He glanced at Dulcy, who looked wildly beautiful in her almost nakedness, and they were still within earshot of the encampment when he heard the shout.

"Somebody woke up and noticed your bay gone," Fargo said. "RIDE!"

He sent the Ovaro into a gallop and Dulcy came

with him as he curved a path through the trees. He stayed north on the mesquite-bush land and took a sharp turn up a low hill and down the left side of it, then swung right again at the bottom. The Mescalero were still unhobbling their horses, he knew, and when they did it would be too dark for them to pick up a trail. He allowed a grim smile as he raced on and cast another glance at Dulcy as she rode, lovely round breasts bouncing in unison, her long, lean body leaning forward, and he wished he had time to stop and take her. She caught his admiring glance and scowled. "Enjoying yourself?" she hissed.

"Definitely," he said and took a sharp curve that made her concentrate on her riding. He continued to ride hard almost through the night, slowing only when he felt the Ovaro beginning to labor. When dawn came up he found a spot where a cluster of pecan trees backed up against a sandstone rock formation and he threaded his way through the trees and into an opening in the rock where a high-sided hollow of stone offered a safe resting place as well as shade. Dulcy swung from the bay, took her clothes from the saddlebag, and slipped into the shirt.

"Why didn't you let me dress back there?" she snapped.

"Is that all you can ask?" he tossed back as he unsaddled the Ovaro.

"It's a start," she returned.

"There's no sound that'll wake a Mescalero quicker than the rustle of cotton and silk," Fargo said. "I wasn't going to risk that."

"You know, that was all your fault," Dulcy said. "If you hadn't insisted on playing Good Samaritan we'd never have been ambushed."

He frowned back at her. "Maybe so," he conceded. "I just wasn't careful enough. I let you upset me."

"By insisting we go on?" Dulcy said with a touch of disdain.

"Yes," he admitted. "I didn't expect that kind of coldness from you."

"You call it coldness. I call it using reason. If I thought those poor devils had a chance to make it I'd have gone along with you," she said.

He turned her answer in his mind but her handsome face held only cool beauty. "I wonder," he said and her small half-shrug was both an acceptance and a dismissal. He studied her with another long glance. "You didn't seem at all surprised to see me," he said.

"I wasn't," she said.

"Why not?" he asked.

"That damn one-track mind of yours. I knew you wouldn't give up bringing me back without one more try," she said, grim annoyance in her voice.

"Aren't you lucky," he grunted and she looked away but not before her eyes had flashed a moment of concession. Fargo took off shirt and jeans and stretched out in the shade of the high rock wall. He watched Dulcy lie down nearby and closed his eyes. The enigma that was Dulcy Abbot had taken on one more facet—fire and ice—he murmured as he let sleep come to him.

He woke with the dawn and hurried on foot from the hiding place, putting on only his gunbelt. Breaking a branch with leaves attached from one of the oaks, he brushed the hoofprints from the ground, moving a hundred yards from the cluster of trees. It was a precaution, yet it was a time for precautions. He didn't believe the Mescalero would follow the prints this far, but they'd pick them up with the new day and trail them for some distance, he was certain. Returning to the rock hollow, he dressed, took the big Sharps from its saddle holster, and climbed higher on the rock formation as Dulcy still slept. When he reached the top he found a spot that let him see over the tops of the oaks into the distance and he settled down to keep a vigil.

Dulcy woke before noon and spotted him high on the rock. She settled down again and waited until he clambered down, satisfied the Apache had given up the trail. "We'll start northwest, circle, and stay away from that damn sandy desert," he said as he led the way from the oaks. "We'll skirt the edge of Edwards Plateau." Dulcy nodded and kept pace with him as he cut across. It was hard riding and when night came there was little energy left for anything but sleep. On the third day, as he headed straight north, he saw the distant expanse of Edwards Plateau come into sight. He swung east and followed the bank of the Rio River and camped one more night alongside the water. By midmorning Fargo saw the rocks bordering Frio Canyon rise in steppelike formations. He paused to let the horses drink despite Dulcy's excited desire to press on, her goal in sight, and she turned a narrow-eyed glance at him.

"You're still angry at me for not agreeing to help those two men, aren't you?" she observed.

"I don't know that angry's the right word," he said.

"What is?" she queried.

"I'm not sure," he frowned. "Maybe it's not being sure of you, of who and what you are."

"I'm somebody who wants to find Harry Kelso and that codicil," she said firmly. "We're more alike than you think. Neither of us gives up."

"Let's ride," he said, unwilling to accept the comparison she had drawn, not yet, anyway. When they reached the edge of Frio Canyon he was surprised at the number of pueblolike cliff dwellings that were occupied by Indian families, mostly Zuni, he guessed from their clothes and the pottery he saw, though they could be Hopi or Acoma. It didn't much matter because he couldn't speak any of the Tanoan languages. They were watched with a mixture of curiosity and wariness as they threaded their way through the adobe village and Dulcy's repeating of Harry Kelso's name drew no response.

They had reached the end of the line of pueblo dwellings when Fargo noted a half-dozen shacks a few hundred yards on and he saw the prospector's marks of shovels, pick-axes, tin pans, and wheelbarrows. He advanced on the first shack at a trot and drew to a halt as a burly, black-bearded figure in overalls and nothing else emerged from the structure. The man stared at him and longer at Dulcy.

"Jesus, what brings you here, strangers? We don't get many visitors here?" he asked.

"We're looking for somebody," Dulcy answered. "Harry Kelso. You know him? Elderly man, almost white hair, tall, thin?"

"Harry Kelso? Sure. He lives just past the bend. What would you want with Harry? He doesn't bother anybody, spends his time doing pottery and basket-weaving, gets along with the Indians real well," the man said.

"I'm an old friend of his," Dulcy explained glibly and hurried her horse forward. Fargo saw the man stare after her, plainly unable to envision her as an old friend of Harry Kelso.

"Much obliged," Fargo said. He hurried after Dulcy and reached her as she rounded the bend in the narrow road. The structure rose up only fifty yards on, a wooden shack built out from one of the adobe pueblo dwellings, a strange grafting of the white man's home onto the ancient redman's shelter. Fargo saw the thin, white-haired figure outside the structure, seated on a wood box and shaping a piece of red clay into a bowl.

The man looked up as Fargo came to a halt and Dulcy swung from the saddle to hurry over to him. "Harry, it's me," she said. Fargo dismounted and stepped closer as Harry Kelso stared at the young woman, his wrinkled face growing more wrinkled as he frowned. "It's me, Dulcy," she repeated and Fargo saw the old man pull his mouth closed as slow recognition swept through him.

"Dulcy," Harry Kelso breathed. "My God, Dulcy."

"That's right, Harry." Dulcy smiled and pressed the old man's arm. "I've come all this way to find you." She turned and gestured to Fargo. "This is my friend, Fargo. He's helped me," she said and Harry Kelso fastened Fargo with a long stare before returning his eyes to Dulcy again.

"You come all this way just to visit, Dulcy?" the man asked.

"Yes, and I need to know something, Harry, something only you know," Dulcy said.

"I don't know anything you'd need knowing," Kelso said.

"But you do. Mother and you were real friends, Harry. She confided in you, trusted you," Dulcy said and Harry Kelso's face softened as he smiled, suddenly plunged into memories of his own.

"Yes, oh yes, we were good friends. She was a fine woman, your mother," he murmured.

"She'd want you to help me. She'd want you to tell me what I need to know," Dulcy said.

"Got nothing to tell, Dulcy," the old man said.

"Yes you do, Harry. Mother added something to her will, something called a codicil and she hid a copy of it," Dulcy said. "She told you where she hid that copy."

"I don't remember," Harry Kelso said and Fargo caught a truculence edging into his voice.

"You think hard about it and you'll remember," Dulcy said. "I know you will. It's real good seeing you again, Harry. I know you wouldn't want me to come all this way for nothing."

"No, I wouldn't want that and it's good seeing you, Dulcy. But I can't remember. It was a long time ago," the man said.

"Not that long ago, Harry," Dulcy said, linking her arm in his. "Show me inside your house. I want to know everything about what you've been doing." She was turning on the charm, insinuating herself and the past into Harry Kelso's present, Fargo saw as the old man rose and started toward the strange, hybrid shack with her. "Why don't you take care of the horses, Fargo," she said with a quick glance backward.

Fargo nodded and led the horses to one side of the structure and unsaddled both as the long shadows of dusk began to move across the land. He went to the house when he finished and stepped inside to find a large front room cluttered with pottery, bowls, vases, and a dozen woven rugs hanging on the walls. "All of this is Harry's work, Fargo. Isn't it wonderful?" Dulcy exuded.

"It is," Fargo said. "Seems you've been happy here, Harry."

"I have, I have," the man said.

"Harry has agreed to think all night and try to remember where Mother hid that codicil," Dulcy said.

"I'm sure when he tries hard enough he'll remember," she added and patted Harry Kelso on his arm, offering him a wide smile of encouragement. But Fargo saw the old man's eyes darken and a stubbornness slide through his face.

"I've room here but it's all taken up, as you can see," Harry Kelso said.

"We'll bed down outside," Dulcy said quickly.

"But I've some fine chili simmering. You could take supper with me," Kelso offered.

"We'd love to," Dulcy said and Fargo had to move two vases to find a spot to sit. The old man dished out the chili on clay plates and it was tasty, accompanied by corn bread he said the Indian women baked in clay ovens. Dulcy kept up a running chatter about old times, her mother, and her regard for Harry but Fargo noted that the old man nodded more than contributed. When the meal was over, Fargo left with Dulcy and found a place on the left side of the house to spread out his bedroll. Dulcy put her blanket beside him and changed into her nightdress in front of him as he watched the long loveliness of her. "Modesty would be silly now, wouldn't it?" she remarked.

"It would," he agreed.

The nightdress pulled on loosely, she settled down beside him. "Is Harry Kelso a gambling man?" she asked smugly. "Who lied to you, me or Rob Abbot?"

"It looks as though Abbot did the lying," Fargo conceded.

"Everything else he told you was a lie," she said and Fargo found himself ready to admit the apparent truth of it. "That's why I have to find that codicil," Dulcy said. "Then I can be rid of Abbot once and for all."

"I hope Harry Kelso remembers," Fargo said.

"He will. I'll keep bringing up things to jog his memory," Dulcy said. She turned on her side and came against him. "You still out of joint about what happened back on the desert?" she asked.

"It's still with me," he admitted.

"So much so you can't screw me?" Dulcy challenged.

"I didn't say that," he answered and she was free of the nightdress in seconds and helping him pull off his clothes. He made love to her and realized he was being harsher and rougher than he needed to be and yet he couldn't seem to pull back. But Dulcy didn't mind. In truth, she responded with her own raw wanting and when her scream pounded into his chest he lay with her coated in perspiration and welcoming sleep in the hot night.

When morning came he found that Harry Kelso had a small well nearby and he washed and dressed and watched Dulcy as she did the same. The old man had coffee on when they went into the house. It was good, strong brew.

"Mexican coatapec," Kelso said, serving a grain biscuit also made by the Indian women.

"You're happy here, Harry," Fargo observed.

"Yep," the old man said. "Lonely sometimes but happy. I'd like more miners stopping by and less Zuni."

"Did you remember, Harry?" Dulcy asked. "Did you think hard during the night?"

"Can't remember," the old man said. "Can't remember."

"You do remember Dulcy's mother making a codicil to her will, don't you?" Fargo questioned.

The old man frowned into space. "Yes, there was something," he said.

"And you remember Mother talking to you about it, telling you where she was going to hide it," Dulcy pressed. "She always said she trusted you more than anybody."

"I remember she always said that. She talked to me about the will but I can't remember anything more," Harry Kelso said. Dulcy shot a glance at Fargo.

"Why don't you explore some and leave me with Harry?" she suggested meaningfully and Fargo shrugged, finished the last of his coffee, and went outside. He walked along the few miners' shacks and found himself passing more pueblo cliff dwellings. The Indians watched him with interest but kept their distance. He halted at an incline and gazed into the distance to see the shape of Frio Canyon. It was a scorching, inhospitable land, unfit for growing much of anything, its beauty bleak and harsh. The shapes and designs on the pueblo Zuni pottery seemed entirely too graceful to grow from the character of its surroundings. He explored further and eventually stretched out beside a sudden stream that appeared as if out of nowhere, generally wasting as much time as he could before he returned to Harry Kelso's house.

Dulcy emerged to meet him, annoyance in her face. "He doesn't remember. We'll have to take him back with us," she said.

"You think going back to your mother's house will jog his memory?" Fargo said.

"I'm sure of it," Dulcy said.

"You told him you want him to go back with you?" Fargo asked.

"No, I want you there. Let's do it now," Dulcy said and Fargo followed her into the house.

"I know how to help you remember, Harry," Dulcy

began. "We're taking you back with us. Being back will make you remember."

The old man turned a frown on Dulcy. "No, no it won't," he said and Fargo heard the instant tightness in his voice. "I'm not going back, no ma'am," Harry Kelso said.

"I'm afraid you'll have to, Harry. I need to find that codicil. I need you to remember where Mother hid it," Dulcy said firmly.

"Mr. Abbot will be there, won't he?" Kelso said and Dulcy nodded. "No, I can't go back. It won't make me remember."

Fargo peered at Harry Kelso. The man was clearly agitated, his eyes troubled. "Why don't you let Harry and me talk alone," Fargo said to Dulcy. She was about to protest but decided not to and hurried out of the house.

Fargo sat down across from the old man and kept his voice gentle. "It's more than not remembering, isn't it, Harry?" he said. Kelso didn't answer but Fargo watched his fingers moving nervously up and down his leg. "You're afraid of something," Fargo said and the silence was becoming an answer. Kelso's eyes averted meeting his and Fargo leaned closer, turning his tone confidential. "Is it Rob Abbot?" he asked. "Are you afraid of Rob Abbot?"

Harry Kelso raised his eyes and Fargo saw the fear in them. "Mr. Abbot's had people killed," the man said.

"Is that what you're afraid of, Harry?" Fargo questioned and Harry shrugged.

"Is that a yes?" Fargo asked and Harry Kelso shrugged again. He was not the kind to play coy, Fargo knew. Yet something stopped him from answering. He balked at a simple admission. Perhaps because things were not so simple, Fargo wondered. "Did you see Rob Abbot destroy the original copy of the codicil?" he asked the man.

"No," Kelso said. He was clear enough about that, Fargo noted.

"Is there something else, Harry? Is there something else you're afraid of?" Fargo asked and Harry Kelso looked away and Fargo saw the implacableness settle over him.

He patted the old man on the arm and went outside where Dulcy leaned against a wall. "He can't remember or he's afraid to remember. Either way it comes out the same," Fargo said. "He as much as said he was afraid of Rob Abbot."

"I don't blame him for that," Dulcy sniffed.

"I just get the feeling there's more he's afraid of," Fargo said. "Or maybe being afraid is part of him now."

"Tell him you'll see that nothing happens to him," Dulcy said and Fargo frowned at her.

"I'm not here to be a damn bodyguard," Fargo protested.

"Don't you want to know the truth? You know Rob Abbot took you in and you know I told you the truth about Harry Kelso. Don't you want to know all of it?" Dulcy asked and he knew she had touched on a truth. He was both curious, angry, and bothered. Answers were not exactly answers. Proof only seemed proof. And Dulcy was still an enigma. He wanted to carry it through, he admitted, if only to himself. He turned and Dulcy went with him into the house where Harry Kelso sat still wrapped in his own darkness.

"I can't remember," he muttered.

"You can and you will, Harry. You owe it to my mother to try. She didn't give you her secret to run away with it. She gave it to you to use, to give me," Dulcy said.

"I had to run," the man said. "I was afraid."

"Of course you were, but you don't have to be afraid anymore. Fargo here will see to that, Harry. We'll take you back and he'll see that nobody does anything to you," Dulcy said.

The man cast a frowning glance up at Fargo. "You'll do that? You promise?" he asked.

"Yes," Fargo said and swore silently. Perhaps it was really only in the old man's mind, a strange, twisted, unfounded fear, he told himself with more hope than confidence.

"I'll help you get your things together, Harry," Dulcy said. "You won't have to do a thing but keep trying to remember." She immediately began to gather clothes into a travel sack and Harry stepped outside with Fargo. They went around to the back of the pueblo section of the house where a gray gelding filled a half-stall with a roofed overhang. Fargo surveyed the horse. It was not an animal for making time, but it was a sturdy mount with a good deep chest and no nobs on its legs and still up on its pasterns.

"What if nothing makes me remember?" Harry Kelso asked him. "Will you see I get to leave?"

"I'll see you get to leave," Fargo said. "And I'm sure Dulcy will pay you for your time and effort." The man nodded, seemingly satisfied with the answer and began to strap his pack onto the gray gelding. Dulcy came out and hung the traveling bag on the lariat strap on the fork swell and then fetched her bay. "I've had enough of Mescaleros. I'm going to try and avoid them as much as I can," Fargo said. "We'll cut straight east to Austin, rest a night there, and go east again to the Brazos. Then we follow the

Brazos all the way north till it passes Fort Worth."
He turned the Ovaro north first, passed the line of
the pueblo dwellings, and then finally headed east,
aware that he'd seldom wanted to finish a job as
much as he did this one.

10

The trip north was slow and Fargo managed to skirt danger throughout the long way. Harry Kelso rode in silence for the most part and stayed close to Fargo, bedding down not more than six feet from him each night, but his eyes grew more and more troubled as they drew closer to Austin. "I didn't expect he'd be a damn chaperon," Dulcy hissed to Fargo one dusk. "I'm going to want you in bed all day when this trip's over."

"That can be arranged," Fargo said and wondered silently why he failed to feel the same way in return. It wasn't like him, he realized, not at all like him. He could only attribute it to the fact that all the unresolved questions that still surrounded Dulcy had intuitively made him draw back. Desire, he was learning, can succumb to caution and uncertainty. But the morning came when he rode to a halt in front of the large slate-roofed house and the corrals and warehouses that spread out beyond it.

Rob Abbot came from the house as Fargo and the others dismounted, his eyes sweeping Dulcy first, with a smile of cold triumph, and then pausing to take in Harry Kelso. His eyes returned to Fargo, narrowed and hard. "What's he doing here?" Abbot asked.

"I brought her gambling man back with her, two

for the price of one," Fargo said and Rob Abbot's eyes grew smaller. "You son of a bitch, you set me up, lied to me from the very start."

"What are you talking about?" Abbot said. "You're not listening to anything she told you, I hope."

"Drop the act. I caught up with Brad Ales along the way," Fargo shot out and Abbot's mouth fell open for an instant. "No wonder you told me not to bother chasing after him."

"Come inside," Abbot said, turning on his heel and striding into the house. Dulcy followed him and Harry Kelso stayed next to Fargo. Inside the spacious living room Abbot turned to Fargo with an apologetic shrug and managed an almost sheepish smile. "Maybe it wasn't exactly the right thing to do but I was desperate," he said. "We can talk about this later, you and I."

"You also sold me a bill of goods on why you wanted Dulcy back," Fargo rasped. "You didn't want her back because you needed her signature on checks. You wanted her back before she could find Harry Kelso."

"I do need her damn signature," Abbot said.

"Maybe but that still wasn't the real reason," Fargo said.

Dulcy's voice cut in, a smug triumph in it. "You hired the right man for the job only he didn't do the right thing for you. It's really quite amusing, Rob," she said.

"Shut up, Dulcy," Abbot snapped.

"Maybe you should all shut up until Harry's memory comes back and we have the copy of that original codicil you burned, Abbot," Fargo said and drew an instant frown from the man.

"What original codicil? What are you talking about, Fargo?" Abbot threw back.

"The one that said Dulcy got control of everything when she turned twenty-one. That's why you burned it," Fargo said.

"Shit, is that what she told you?" Abbot said. "I never burned any original codicil. We know she made one but nobody could find it."

Fargo's eyes went to Dulcy, who looked uncomfortable. "Is that so? You never had hold of the original codicil?" he asked.

"But there is one," Dulcy said.

"But you never saw it. You don't know what's in it, neither of you do," Fargo said and her silence was an admission. "Goddammit, you lied to me, too. You don't know that it gives you control at twenty-one."

"I'm sure it does," Dulcy said.

"The hell you are," Fargo said. "You brought Harry to remember where it was hidden so you could find out what was in it."

"And he had you bring me back to stop me from that," Dulcy said, flashing a glance at Abbot. "He's afraid of what's in it. He wants the will to stand as it is."

"I believe in being prudent," Abbot said.

"You believe in getting rid of anyone who stands in your way," Dulcy threw at Abbot.

"So do you, my dear," Abbot said.

"You're both damn liars and you're both afraid of what's in that codicil and maybe you're a lot more," Fargo said.

"Nonsense. Don't listen to him, Fargo," Dulcy said.

"You brought her back, Fargo. Here's the rest of your pay. You can take off, now," Abbot said, drawing a sheaf of bills from his pocket and handing it to Fargo.

"No, you can't leave me," Harry Kelso said as his hand pulled at Fargo's arm. "You promised you'd take care of me."

Fargo took Abbot's money and pushed it into his pocket. "I sure as hell earned this," he said and turned to the old man. "And I'm not throwing you to the wolves, Harry. I don't like being set up, played for a damn fool, my neck put on the line. I want to know the truth myself and I'm going to find out what it is."

"I think that's wonderful, just what I want," Dulcy said warmly.

"I think you ought to mind your own business, Fargo," Rob Abbot muttered.

"It was my neck then and it's my business now," Fargo said as he took Harry Kelso's arm. "Let's take a walk through the house, Harry," he said.

"I'm ordering you out, Fargo," Abbot said. "You're on my property."

"It's my property, too," Dulcy put in. "You go with Fargo, Harry." Fargo shot her a glance. She was certainly keeping up her role as an enigma. He took Harry Kelso into the next room, a study, and let the old man's eyes roam every corner of it.

"Clara . . . Mrs. Abbot . . . and I used to sit and talk here," he murmured.

"Take your time, Harry," Fargo said.

Harry nodded, slowly scanned the room again. "We used to talk a lot in the kitchen, too. She was a good woman," he said.

"Let's visit the kitchen," Fargo said and heard doors slamming shut beyond the living room. He visited most of the rooms at the right side of the house with Harry and when night fell he left with the old man and set his bedroll down a dozen yards from the house. Harry came down on his blanket alongside him.

"Can't remember," Harry murmured.

"Take your time. We've more rooms to visit tomorrow," Fargo said and began to shed his clothes. Harry Kelso undressed and slept almost at once as Fargo munched on a dried beef strip. He had started to sleep when he heard the door open and saw Dulcy come toward him from the house. She knelt down at the edge of the bedroll and wore a filmy pink nightgown.

"I know you don't know what to really believe anymore," she began.

"Bull's-eye, honey, especially about you," Fargo growled.

"I'll make you believe. I just need a little more time. You keep on with Harry," Dulcy said.

"Count on it," Fargo said.

She leaned forward and took his hand and cupped it around her breasts. "This will be waiting for you. I'll make up for everything, you wait and see. Unless you want to come into my room now."

"I'll wait and see," Fargo said and pulled his hand back. She offered him a warm smile and hurried back to the house. He lay back wishing he could come to some conclusion about her and pulled sleep around himself.

When morning came he found coffee and bacon waiting inside the house, along with Dulcy, who smiled sweetly. Rob Abbot appeared and scowled. Harry Kelso enjoyed breakfast.

"I could get some of my men and throw you out of here," Abbot threatened.

"You could get a lot of people hurt, maybe dead," Fargo said. "Besides, you're in the cat-bird seat. Harry can't make his memory work and you're home free."

"I don't favor taking that chance," Abbot said.

"Your call, then," Fargo said, ice suddenly coating his words, and Abbot stalked from the room mumbling to himself. Fargo spent the rest of the day moving through the house with Harry Kelso, room to room, cellar to attic, and when night came he sat beside the old man outside once again. Harry Kelso mumbled apologetically but Fargo saw more fear than anything else in his eyes. "What is it, Harry? Why are you so afraid? I'm between you and Abbot," he said.

"I keep thinking about Tommy Matthews," the old man said, running a hand through his white hair.

"Who the hell is Tommy Matthews?" Fargo frowned.

"He worked for Clara, as her stableboy. She trusted Tommy, too," Harry said.

"Why are you thinking about him?" Fargo questioned.

"When Miss Clara finished that new piece to her will she called in Tommy and told him to ride to Wichita Falls and bring her lawyers back to see her," Harry said. "Only Tommy never reached Wichita Falls. They found him killed a few thousand yards from the house."

"Somebody heard her tell Tommy what she wanted him to do. They figured she'd have her lawyers come only if she'd made a codicil to her will and they made sure the message was never delivered," Fargo said.

"Yes, yes that's how it happened because it was the next day, after they found Tommy, that she told me she was going to hide that new part to her will," Harry Kelso said.

"You think it was Abbot who overheard Clara and killed Tommy?" Fargo queried.

"He was here," the old man said. "And so was Dulcy."

Fargo turned the words in his mind. It was growing clear why Harry Kelso was afraid. He didn't know who to fear. "That's why you left soon after, isn't it, Harry?" Fargo asked and the old man nodded. "All of this has come back to you. Can't you remember more? When Tommy Matthews was killed she told you where she was going to hide the codicil. Where, Harry, think back. Where?"

Harry Kelso lay back but his wrinkled forehead was heavily creased in thought. "She was afraid, too. She wanted to hide it until she could find a chance to get to her lawyers. But she had the heart attack first and that was the end," Kelso thought aloud.

"You don't have to be afraid now, Harry. Think hard. You must remember something," Fargo said, even as he knew that can congeal the mind.

"Someplace nobody would look she told me," Harry Kelso was saying and Fargo knelt closer to catch every word of the old man's mutterings. "Smoke, I thought when she talked. Smoke and fire," Harry said. "Can't remember more."

"Smoke and fire," Fargo repeated as he frowned. What did it mean, he pondered. Smoke and fire. Someplace where there was smoke and fire. But hell, they usually went together. It could mean anyplace, he scowled and then caught himself. No, not anyplace. Smoke and fire didn't go together in a barn or a tree or a bathroom. They went together on a hearth and on a stove, but what did that mean? He turned to Kelso again and shook the old man. "Why did you think smoke and fire when she told you what she was going to do? Remember, dammit, try harder," he said.

"I told her there could be smoke and fire. I remember saying that. But she said it'd be safe," Harry said.

"Even though there'd be smoke and fire the codicil would be safe," Fargo frowned. "That meant she was going to put it into something, a steel box." He halted, suddenly on his feet as thoughts exploded through his mind. "Inside a chimney. A steel box inside a chimney," he hissed, excitement surging through him. "There'd be smoke and fire going up a chimney."

He saw Harry Kelso staring at him, his eyes opened wide. "Yes, that was it. She told me she was going to hide it in the chimney. It's all coming back now," the old man said and pushed himself to his feet. "Oh God, yes, yes."

"There's a fireplace in the living room. Anywhere else?" Fargo questioned.

"No, except for one in the kitchen but that's too small, only for the stoves. She wouldn't have put it there," Harry said.

"Let's go find a ladder," Fargo said. "You try the barn. I'll try that toolshed." He hurried off, moving silently though the house was dark and silent. He found a long ladder in the toolshed and a long-handled rake and carried them to the rear of the house. He had just set the ladder at a proper angle when Harry Kelso returned and held the bottom as Fargo began to climb, the rake in his hand. The ladder reached within four feet of the slate roof and he was able to pull himself the rest of the way by taking hold of the rain gutters.

He lay flat on the roof for a moment, the rake still clutched beside him, and began to crawl on his stomach toward the chimney. He crawled slowly, taking care not to scrape along the slate tiles, and rose to his feet only when he was beside the chimney. He reached the long-handled rake into the black opening of the chimney, reached lower and let the rake move from side to side across the stones. Suddenly he felt it catch on something and he moved it again. The teeth of the rake were striking against a narrow protrusion, a small piece of stone jutting out from the others, and then he felt the rake strike against something that moved, swayed. He uttered a sound of triumph. The rake moved against a chain that swayed when he touched it.

Maneuvering the teeth of the rake carefully, he made at least three attempts before he got two of the teeth to catch on to the chain. He began to draw the chain upward, ever so slowly so as not to dislodge his precarious hold on it. When he saw the blackened chain appear near the top of the chimney, he reached down with his hand, grasped hold of it, and began to pull it up. He rose to his feet as he drew the chain up and had to force the shout to stay in his throat as the small steel box appeared at the end of the chain. He lowered it to the roof and stared at it for a moment. The soot-covered steel box was tightly attached to the chain and would take a metal saw to cut it free. But there was no lock on the box, he noticed, and he pressed the latch with his hands and the lid came open.

He wiped his hands on his jeans before lifting the neatly rolled curl of paper from inside the box. He opened it just enough to see there was a short, accompanying letter with it. He carefully put the curled papers inside his shirt and carefully slid along the slate roof to where the ladder waited. He eased himself onto the top rung and climbed down to meet Harry Kelso's waiting eyes. "Got it," he said.

"By God," Harry breathed.

"We haven't light enough to read it here," Fargo said.

"I don't want to read it, Fargo," Harry Kelso said. "I've done my part. I just want to get away from here. I want to start back." Fear still haunted the man's eyes, Fargo saw.

"You have done your part, Harry. You go your way and good luck. It's a long trip," Fargo said.

"I've done it before. I'll do it again. Nobody bothers an old man riding alone, not even the Mescalero," Harry said.

Fargo shook his hand and watched him gather his things onto the gray gelding and ride slowly away with a backward wave of his hand. Fargo settled down onto the top of his bedroll and shed his clothes and tucked the codicil under his shirt.

He rose with the morning sun, washed at the well near one of the bunkhouses, and walked to the main house when he saw Dulcy in the doorway, "Coffee?" she asked.

"Sounds good," he said and went into the house with her, where Abbot glared at him.

"Where's Harry?" Dulcy asked.

"Gone," Fargo said as he sipped the coffee and enjoyed the astonishment mixed with alarm that seized Abbot and Dulcy.

"What do you mean, gone?" Dulcy snapped, finding her voice.

"He wanted to go back."

"And you let him? After all the trouble I went through to bring him back here?" Dulcy almost shouted.

"He came through. He had a right to go his way," Fargo said and drew the codicil from inside his shirt.

"You found it," Dulcy gasped, wide-eyed.

"Inside the chimney," Fargo said.

"I'll take that," Abbot said.

"Hell you will." Fargo smiled. Abbot took a step forward, his hand dropping to his gun menacingly. Fargo's smile widened. "I didn't know you wanted to commit suicide," he said and Abbot's hand dropped to his side as he stepped backward. "That's better. Now we'll do a little reading," Fargo said and uncurled the codicil. "She has a letter with it," he said and began to read:

The Firm of Bosworth & Calkins
Cedar Street
Wichita Falls, Texas.

I have made a codicil to my will. Please arrange to visit with me regarding this matter at your earliest convenience.

Respectfully,
Clara Abbot

Fargo put the letter aside. "This is a copy of the letter she gave Tommy Matthews to deliver," he said.

"Where'd you hear about Tommy Matthews?" Abbot shot out.

"Harry Kelso had to tell him, stupid," Dulcy said scathingly and Fargo held up the codicil.

"Now for the important part," he said and began to read again:

Codicil

To the last will and testament of Clara Abbot of Fort Worth, Texas. Please be it known that by this codicil I change, alter, and supersede the terms of my will, dated March 10, 1856.

Because of information I have received which proves that my husband, Rob Abbot, is a thief, scoundrel, and totally abominable person, and because my only daughter, Dulcy, continues to be an unprincipled, selfish, uncaring, and vicious young woman, I hereby state that neither of them shall have any rights to or interest in Abbot Enterprises.

I hereby give you as my solicitors power of attorney to liquidate all the assets of Abbot Enterprises, and divide the cash returns among all the employees of Abbot Enterprises working there at the time of my death, except Rob Abbot and Dulcy Abbot.

These are my final desires as so stated.

Clara Abbot

Fargo lowered the codicil, folding it this time and putting it into his pocket. "You lose, both of you, and I'd say there is justice in the world," Fargo said. "You didn't know what was in that codicil but you were willing to lie, cheat, use people, and kill to get your hands on it."

"He had you bring me back here so he could get rid of me when he couldn't find the codicil," Dulcy accused.

"And you went to find Harry Kelso so you could get hold of the codicil and get rid of me," Abbot snapped back.

"It doesn't much matter, now," Fargo said, taking the last sip of his coffee.

"How much do you want for it?" Abbot asked as Fargo turned and started for the door.

"Not for sale," Fargo said.

"What are you going to do with it?" Dulcy asked.

"Take it to Bosworth and Calkins. That's what Clara wanted. I think she deserves that," Fargo said. "So does Tommy Matthews."

He walked from the house, casting a backward glance at Abbot. The man was the kind who'd not pause to shoot him in the back. But Abbot made no move and Fargo stepped outside, gathered his things, and saddled the Ovaro. He rode away with a last glance at the buildings and stock of Abbot Enterprises, turned the Ovaro north, and headed for Wichita Falls.

He rode slowly, a sour taste in his mouth, and he knew he had hoped something would happen to clear Dulcy of suspicion, something that would have restored his faith in her. But that hadn't happened. Harry Kelso hadn't known who to fear and Fargo realized he hadn't known in whom to believe. The sourness stayed inside him as he rode and when night came he bedded down under a black oak half surrounded by three other trees. He put out his bedroll, unsaddled the pinto, and rested his back against the saddle as he stretched out.

But he kept his gunbelt on and the moon rose and he watched it slide across the night sky when his ears caught the sound, a horse slowly approaching. He didn't move but his hand came to rest on the butt of the big Colt. His eyes were on the passage between two of the oaks as the horse and rider appeared and came closer. Fargo saw the lean, tall figure swing to the ground. "I had to come," she said, stepping to him and dropping to her knees.

"Had to?"

"Yes, to make you see it's not just what it seems. I want you to know there was more, from the moment we met," she said. "And I want you to know that I understand what you're doing."

"Good."

"I want to prove that to you," Dulcy said as she unbuttoned her shirt and flung the garment aside. The lovely, round-cupped breasts beckoned to him.

She rose, pulled off her skirt and slip, and stood with a kind of defiant pride in front of him, then came down to her knees again and her mouth was on his, her breasts pressing into his hands. "Please, once more, for me, for us," she murmured. She was unbuttoning his shirt, unsnapping his jeans and he took his gunbelt off and tossed it aside, swept up by the beautiful hunger of her, the touch of her warm, tingling flesh. "Oh Jesus," Dulcy said, spreading herself over him, rubbing her fluffy nap across his groin.

He lifted for her, let her warm portal press against him but she held back thrusting over him and continued to smother him with her body, her breasts pressed into his face. He heard the voice as if it were far away for a moment and then realized it wasn't far away at all. "That's enough," it said and Dulcy rolled from him with a quick, graceful motion, her tight rear flipping into the air as she scooped up her shirt and skirt. Fargo stared at Rob Abbot and the Remington the man held trained on him, a five-shot single-action piece.

"It took you long enough," he heard Dulcy snap and turned to stare at her as she pulled her skirt on. He couldn't help a wry smile from touching his lips.

"Birds of a feather," he murmured.

"We decided we had to cooperate with each other," Dulcy said.

"Getting that damn codicil was first," Abbot said tightly and Fargo glanced at the man and back to Dulcy. They had made a quick marriage of convenience. The ties were far from strong.

"You get rid of me, first. Then one of you gets rid of the other," Fargo said.

"We're going to work together," Dulcy said.

"Who are you trying to kid? Not me. I don't need

kidding," Fargo said, flicking a glance at the Colt where it lay in his gunbelt. "You're still trying to kid each other that you're going to be partners. Don't make me laugh."

"Shut up, Fargo," Rob Abbot shouted and Fargo tossed a grin at Dulcy. He smiled again as he saw the flash of suspicion touch her eyes. Abbot started toward where Fargo had tossed his jacket. "I'll get the codicil," he said.

"No, I'll get it. You watch him," Dulcy said.

"No, goddammit, I'll get it," Abbot snapped and Fargo let out a guffaw.

"This is real good. You don't even trust each other enough to get something out of my jacket," he roared.

"Dammit, I'll get it," Dulcy said and rushed forward to scoop up the jacket a second before Abbot reached it.

"Give me the goddam jacket," Abbot shouted at her. "Don't you see what he's doing?" But the man had turned to Dulcy in his fury and Fargo rolled, flinging himself as hard and fast as he could. His body hit Rob Abbot in the ankles and the man fell backward over him, a shot going wild into the air. Fargo's hand shot out and yanked the Colt from the holster on the ground. He saw Abbot firing from on his back. Fargo half rolled again and the shot hurtled past him and Dulcy's screamed gasp of pain followed it instantly.

He cast a glance at her and saw her collapsing, her abdomen turning red. Abbot had paused, his eyes on her for an instant, but time enough for Fargo to whirl again and fire as Abbot brought his gun up. The shot slammed into the man's forehead and Fargo put his head down to avoid the explosion of blood and bone that showered through the air. He crawled backward and pushed to his feet, at Dulcy's side in two long steps. "Damn," he murmured as he stared down at her. She had already ceased to breathe. He gently placed her shirt over her face and turned away and gathered his things. He was riding north before the moon dipped below the horizon.

He'd reach Wichita Falls by morning to finish an obligation to a woman he'd never met. Justice would be done, but sometimes it took some strange twists along the way.

LOOKING FORWARD!
The following is the opening
section from the next novel in the exciting
Trailsman **series from Signet:**

THE TRAILSMAN #148
CALIFORNIA QUARRY

California, 1860 . . .
where the glitter of El Dorado
made Argonauts of dreamers and deserters,
enslaving desperate men
in a golden cage of cruelty and madness.

The Busted Bottle Saloon in San Francisco was the rowdiest groggery west of the Mississippi, Fargo thought as he ducked a flying chair which hit the wall behind him and splintered into a hundred pieces. Or east of it, for that matter. Fargo hunched alongside the bar and found himself nose to nose with the red-faced bartender as a flying bottle smashed the mirror and shards of glass showered them.

"Second time this week," the bartender muttered, nodding toward the busted mirror above the long gleaming mahogany bar. He took a long pull on the bottle of red-eye in his fist, then caught Fargo's gaze and offered it to him. Fargo shook his head.

Fargo eased up slowly and peered over the edge of the bar, his hand on his Colt. The brawl between a table of rowdy sailors and some equally contentious prospectors seemed to be winding down. No reason to get in the middle of somebody else's pointless fracas, thought Fargo. Especially since he just came in for a quiet drink to kill some time before the Golden Lily docked.

The sailors were beating a hasty retreat out the door, hurling taunts and an occasional chair toward the rugged gold diggers. The other patrons of the bar were slowly emerging from behind upended tables as the noise died down. The prospectors settled themselves around a large table and the bartender stood. Fargo took his place again at the bar and hooked one boot on the foot railing.

"What'll it be?" the bartender asked, smoothing the wisps of hair over his balding pate. "Just got a case of fine brandy. Came by clipper round the Horn. Make you a nice brandy punch, brandy sling, maybe."

"Straight," Fargo said. He turned around slowly and his lake blue eyes surveyed the large room of The Broken Bottle. Seemed like every lowlife ruffian, thief, cutthroat and two-bit criminal ended up in the city of the Golden Gate. Two wool-scarfed bruisers, from back East by the look of them, hunched over the bar with half-empty bottles in their meaty fists. A table of swarthy-looking desperadoes in colorfully striped wool serapes played a hostile game of poker. Four big sunburned dandies huddled in a corner talking loudly and Fargo, catching their accent, guessed they were convicts fresh from Australia.

A small dapper man in a checked vest drew his

attention. His face was pinched like a mouse's and his handlebar mustache drooped disconsolately. He glided among the tables, stopping here and there to talk to someone, always patting him on the back or grasping the back of the chair. Fargo wondered who the strange little man was.

Fargo watched as the man leaned over to speak to someone and his small hand slipped inside the man's coat pocket. There was a momentary flash of gold as the small fellow straightened up again, tipped his hat, and moved along. A pickpocket, Fargo thought. And a damned good one, too. Lifting pocket watches and everything else. He watched as the pickpocket lifted several more items. Fargo had just decided to move toward him when the little man slipped out the bat-wing doors and onto the crowded street. Fargo shrugged and turned toward the back of the barroom.

The faro and monte tables were hopping with business. Dice and gold coins clattered dully across the boards on the blue cloth tables. An occasional roar of the gathered crowd greeted winners and losers alike.

Fargo took a swig of his brandy and swirled it around in his mouth. Damn fine. San Francisco was known for having the purest liquors, the best cigars, the best guns and bowie knives of any city in the West.

"That'll be three dollars," the bartender said.

Only trouble was, Fargo thought wryly as he fished the money out of his pocket, you paid for it. Since '49, when gold had flooded in from the hills, San Francisco had been a boomtown with booming prices to boot. It had the finest everything available at the highest prices. Only thing the city didn't have was enough women.

Fargo finished the brandy and made his way toward the gaming tables. As he drew near, a flash of green silk caught his eye. He saw the form of a pert blonde in a low-cut gown, dyed ostrich feathers in her high piled hair. She stood leaning over the table. Her décolletage exposed most of her breasts and her deep cleavage was stuffed with bills and coins.

"Blow on 'em, Lucky Lucy," a greasy-haired man was saying. He was holding up dice before her face with one hand. With the other, he stuffed a dollar down her dress. He didn't remove his hand quickly, either. The woman raised her head and Fargo saw her familiar blue eyes and arched brows.

Surprise hit him like a cold wave. Lucy Thomas. Lucy Thomas here in the grimiest gin mill in Frisco. He never would have believed it if he hadn't seen it himself. She sure had come a long way from the prosperous farm in Missouri where he'd last seen her.

Lucy puckered her lips and then spotted Fargo. He smiled and nodded to her. She blanched, hesitated just a moment, then blew on the dice. The greaser yelped his delight and the throng bellowed as he threw. Lucy straightened up and whirled away, plunging into the crowd.

"Snake eyes?!" the man screamed in dismay. The crowd laughed.

Fargo pushed through the mob after her. His keen nose caught the faint whiff of her perfume among the booze and the far less appealing odors in the crowded bar. A door opened and closed ahead of him. He pushed through another group of men and came up to it. A big bullish type stepped astride the door.

"Where do you think you're going?" he asked.

Excerpt from CALIFORNIA QUARRY

"I know that lady," Fargo said.

The bull gave a chuckle.

"You and a thousand other guys," he said.

Fargo shrugged. Well, Lucy Thomas had seen him and recognized him. And if she didn't want to say hello, then that was her affair. He turned away disappointed, then glanced up at the large clock over the bar. Nearly three.

The Golden Lily would be docking before the wind died at sunset. But tides might bring it in early or late. He'd better get a move on. Fargo left the stuffiness of The Broken Bottle, glad to step out into the clear fresh July air. He hastened down Lombard Street toward the docks, thinking of the fresh-faced farmgirl he'd known as Lucy Thomas.

An hour later, Fargo was still waiting. He leaned against a wooden keg opposite the bustling Embarcadero. Behind him loomed the sandy wind-swept hills of San Francisco, a steep jumble of shacks and shanties, fine board houses with bay windows, and occasional adobe huts and canvas tents. Before him, the wharf swarmed with burly dockmen. A dense forest of tall masts creaked and swayed, the ropes and ends of rolled sails snapping. The stiff wind of early March whipped the white-capped waves of the harbor. A three-masted clipper, sails slackened, eased toward the wooden dock. Even at this distance, Fargo could read the name on the clipper's bow. And it wasn't the right one.

The ship, sails slack, eased toward the dock. The decks were crowded with Chinese in blue trousers and tunics and flat straw hats. The dockworkers slung ropes out to make the ship fast and soon the gangplanks were in place. The swarm of blue-clothed Chinese swarmed onto shore. Two swells in suits, swinging their canes grandly, passed close by.

"A lot of celestials coming through these days," one sniffed.

Fargo had heard many people refer to the Chinese as celestials, which came from their own name for their country, the Celestial Empire.

"Escaping the latest war," the other answered before they passed out of hearing.

The newspapers were full of stories about how the British and its allies had taken over Canton and continued to import opium into the gigantic country, to the dismay of the mandarins.

To one side of the dock stood a line of wagons with tall enclosed wooden sides. A huge man with jet black curly hair, carrying a braided leather quirt, jumped down off the first wagon and approached the ship, holding a large sign written in Chinese characters. The celestials mobbed him, babbling questions. The man waved them toward the wagons, where other men jumped down and began to herd the Chinese inside the wagons.

The ship was empty of celestials when Fargo noticed a young woman descending the gangplank alone. She was small, but willowy beneath her loose blue trousers, and moved with a delicate gait. Her long black hair, blown by the March wind, glistened in the sun. Her almond eyes were large and perplexed. She appeared to be looking for someone. She reached the end of the gangplank, and stood, hesitating and confused, as the other Chinese moved away from the ship and toward the wagons.

Three big dockworkers noticed and moved toward her. Fargo could tell they were up to no good. He crossed the planked dock just as one of them, a redhead with a flushed face, made a grab for the young woman.

The young woman tried to cry out, but the redhead had his hand clamped over her mouth. No one else seemed to take any notice. The redhead slung her over his shoulder and headed toward cover between the huge piles of crates and barrels on the dock. The two other men followed.

Fargo quickened his step, heading to the other side of the crates so he could come up behind them. Just as he rounded the corner, he collided with the dapper pickpocket he had seen in The Butsted Bottle. The man's long mustache twitched and his eyes registered curiosity as Fargo hastily pushed him aside.

Fargo slowed as he angled around the mountain of crates and barrels. He slid between the stacks. A man laughed and he heard her low moan, protesting.

Fargo stepped out from cover and saw the three men holding the woman. The redhead reached over and ripped her tunic from top to bottom. Her small round breasts were dark-tipped. She seemed to go limp. The big man began to unbutton his pants.

"Let her go," Fargo said.

The men's heads whipped around at the unexpected voice. The carrot-top's face grew redder when he saw Fargo standing there.

"Mind your own business, stranger," he growled. The other two men glared at Fargo. The young woman glanced up at Fargo with surprise and hope.

"I said, let her go."

At this, the redhead grabbed the woman as the two other men came barreling straight at Fargo. He dodged at the last second and stuck out a foot as the tall skinny one approached. The man tripped and went down onto the planks of the dock, hard. He groaned and didn't stir again. Fargo spun around and hit the second, a heavyset short man, hard in the gut. The man's breath left him in a *swoosh* and he staggered back into a pile of crates. Fargo followed it with an uppercut to the chin, which bounced his head and he slumped down.

Fargo turned toward the redhead holding the small woman in his big paws. He flung her aside and she hit the dock and rolled a few times. Fargo lunged forward, catching the big man in the middle. They crashed into the stack of crates which tumbled down around them as Fargo rained punches and blows on the man. In a few moments, it was over.

Fargo pushed the crates aside and stood up. The three men lay groaning among the splinters of crates. Fargo shook his head to clear it and looked around. The Chinese woman was nowhere to be seen.

Fargo got to his feet and emerged from the piles of crates. At the end of the dock, the high-sided wagons into which he had seen the celestials being herded were closed tight. The huge man with ebony hair climbed aboard the lead wagon. Then he whipped his mules, hard. The line of wagons started forward, heading down the Embarcadero. It was likely she had gone into a wagon with the other Chinese, Fargo thought.

Fargo wiped his face on his sleeve.

"Hey. That was some fight," a voice said from just next to his elbow. The checkered vested pickpocket stood alongside him. "You always take on three at once?"

Fargo looked quizzically at the small man, who seemed to materialize from nowhere.

"If that's all that's available," Fargo answered, taking a step back. "And keep out of my pockets."

The little man grinned, held up his small hands in the air, and wiggled his fingers.

"Name's Billy Shears," he said.

"Skye Fargo."

"Um," Billy said with keen interest. "I know all about you. Famous man, the Trailsman. Can outrun anybody. Find his way through the roughest terrain."

Fargo checked his pockets. His money was still there.

"I put it back already," Billy said with a wink.

Fargo laughed.

Billy glanced along the Embarcadero and his face suddenly paled. "It's been fine meeting you, Mr. Skye Fargo," he added.

Fargo looked toward the crowded street and saw two coppers sauntering along the wooden wharf, spinning their nightsticks. When Fargo looked again at the spot where Billy Shears had stood, it was empty. The little pickpocket had simply vanished.

The two policemen stopped to ask questions of several bystanders and soon made their way over to Fargo.

"We're looking for an individual who's been sighted on the docks," one of the coppers said, after tipping his round-topped hat. His description left no doubt in Fargo's mind that they were looking for Shears.

"Yeah," Fargo said. "He was around here a minute ago. But, I didn't see which way he went."

The officers looked disappointed.

"When we get our hands on him this time," one said menacingly, "he'll be sorry. We've made arrangements with the military to put him out on Alcatraz." Fargo had seen the square form of the military prison on the desolate island far out in the bay.

The two policemen continued up the wharf, stopping to ask others if they had seen which way the short pickpocket had fled.

A schooner out in the harbor was loosening its sails and heading in. The masthead was a blond mermaid with painted pink breasts. Next to it, Fargo read the name inscribed on the bow—THE GOLDEN LILY. So, Professor Ross Flyte was arriving at last.

In a few minutes, the ship had been made fast and the passengers were descending the gangplank. The ship's crew unloaded large wooden crates and trunks. A spry man in a frock coat and a canvas explorer's helmet bounded down the wooden incline. Fargo hastened forward.

"You must be Professor Flyte," Fargo said, extending his hand.

"Mr. Fargo!" the man said, his eyes crinkling with pleasure. He removed his hat and his wispy gray hair was tousled by the breeze. "Thank you for meeting my ship. Did you get my instructions?"

"I got the message that you needed a wagon to transport a bunch of wooden crates. Something about a collection," Fargo said. "Is that wagon big enough?"

Fargo nodded toward the corner of Lombard Street where a heavy mountain wagon with eight mules stood waiting. Fargo's black-and-white pinto stood tethered nearby, gleaming in the sun.

"Yes!" Ross Flyte said. "That wagon will be perfect! And I have the first installment of your payment right here." Ross handed Fargo an envelope fat with bills.

"Just what kind of cargo is this?" Fargo asked. But just then, Flyte noticed two of the crew tossing a wooden box off the ship.

"No! No! Be careful with that!" the professor shouted, hastening toward them, and Fargo was left with his question unanswered.

Whatever it was, the crates were valuable to Ross Flyte, Fargo thought as he moved toward Lombard Street to bring the mountain wagon toward the dock. The professor had offered a lot of money—four thousand dollars—to hire Skye Fargo to meet his ship and haul a wagonload overland from San Francisco to St. Louis. It was damned good money. Even for a tough and long haul.

By the time Fargo brought the wagon next to the Golden Lily, dozens of wooden crates were piled on the dock, all stamped "R. Flyte—USA." Fargo tethered the lead mule and his Ovaro.

For the next hour, the dock was chaotic with crates and swarming with workers as they packed the wagon, piling the crates high and lashing a canvas top over them. Flyte seemed to be everywhere at once, shouting instructions to the dockworkers, enjoining them to take care not to drop the crates.

In all the flurry, there was no time to talk. There would be plenty of that during the long trip to St. Louis. But Fargo had a chance to study Flyte and he liked what he saw. The old man's creased face seemed open and honest. Behind the wire-rimmed spectacles, his brown eyes shone with intelligence. From his clothing, well cut but not flashy, Fargo knew he came from some wealth.

An hour before sunset, the wagon was loaded and the canvas cover tied down.

"We can spend the night in Frisco," Fargo said, "or head out on the last ferry and make a couple of hours before we camp. What's your pleasure?"

"I'm eager to get going," Ross responded.

Fargo nodded. It suited him fine not to spend another night in the dangerous wilds of the Golden Gate City. They boarded the wagon and Fargo took the reins and the mules started down Lombard Street.

They had just passed The Broken Bottle when Fargo heard a familiar voice.

"Let me go!" a woman's voice shrieked. It was Lucy Thomas.

"The hell I will," a gruff voice said.

Fargo halted the mules and peered down a dark alleyway next to the bar. He saw an opened doorway and, framed in it, two struggling forms. Fargo headed the wagon into the deserted alley and tossed the reins to Ross. He leapt down, reaching the doorway in a few swift strides.

A fat, oily man with pig eyes held Lucy. She squirmed in his pudgy white hands. She wore a traveling cape over her green silk dress and clutched a small valise.

"I spent plenty of money on you," the man said.

"Let her go," Fargo muttered, stepping up to them.

The oily man barely gave him a glance. Lucy jumped to see him there and then blushed.

"Push off, stranger. This is none of your affair."

"The lady is a friend of mine," Fargo said. "So it is my business."

Fargo drew his Colt slowly and cocked it for effect. The fat man's eyes narrowed and he clutched Lucy closer to him.

"You don't know who you're fooling with, stranger."

Fargo was surprised the fat man could move so fast, but the silver-carved pistol was in his hand in an instant as Fargo dived to one side. The shot split the air where he'd been standing a moment before. Fargo hit the dirt and rolled once, coming to his feet. The pig-eyed man held Lucy in front of him as a shield.

"Move off," the man said. "She's staying here. Ain't you?"

He shook her roughly. Lucy didn't meet Fargo's eyes, but nodded her head.

Fargo bent down to retrieve his hat, his eyes scanning for an opening, a clear shot. But there wasn't one. He beat the hat against his thigh to get the dust out, then donned it. He turned away, intending to lull the man into relaxing his guard. Fargo started back toward the waiting wagon, ears alert.

And then he heard it—the faint click of the trigger.

And Lucy Thomas screamed.

There's an epidemic with 27 million victims. And no visible symptoms.

It's an epidemic of people who can't read.

Believe it or not, 27 million Americans are functionally illiterate, about one adult in five.

The solution to this problem is you... when you join the fight against illiteracy. So call the Coalition for Literacy at toll-free **1-800-228-8813** and volunteer.

Volunteer Against Illiteracy. The only degree you need is a degree of caring.